QUEEN CITY HUSTLAS

More Than A Hood Romance

JAETENE

Mz. Lady P Presents, LLC

Queen City Hustlas

Chapter One

OCTAVIA MILLS

S itting in Mrs. Pittman's class trying to figure out what my next move was going to be. My name is Octavia Mills, and I am seventeen and about to graduate from Dudley High School. With it being such a big school, I guess people assumed I had a mob of friends, but I don't even have a handful. I was popular, but only because I was dating Omari Jordan, the star quarterback for DHS. It was a handful dealing with his various females and keeping his image. I swear I was tired of trying with his ass.

Taking Omari's mess wasn't a must, and I was a now seeing it was a choice. I was far from ugly with my smooth dark brown skin that was proudly blemished free. I am a size eighteen and still pull mad attention. It doesn't faze me one bit cause these boys only to want to fuck and that's Omari's main issue. He stays bugging me about when we gonna take that step, and I just don't think he will ever get the importance of it to me.

With all the unwanted attention, the only girls I hang with are my best friend Santana and her sister, Soraya Lee. Santana and I also have another friend Kimbella Williams who Soraya didn't like because Bella had no filter and rarely held her tongue. Like me Bella was thick, but she carried it well. Just like with me, it brought the unwanted pulls at the arm or the "Aye come 'ere quick" that dudes like to scream.

Rolling my eyes at the thought, I saw that class was almost over, and I needed to get with my girls to make sure our graduation plans and moves were still in motion.

DIINNGG DIIINNGG

Hearing the bell, I knew I grabbed my book bag and headed to find Santana and Kimbella so that I could let them in on some tea. See with graduation approaching, Omari is, of course, throwing a kickback. Mari parents were rarely home, and I met them maybe five times within the two years we have been together. His mom was beautiful for her age, and his dad complimented her slay because he was just as fine. They never struck me as the family type. They enjoyed me because Omari enjoyed me. Catching up to Santana by her locker, I could tell she had more tea than me.

"Ewww fix your face. What's wrong, Tana?" I asked, pulling out my phone and ignoring Omari's call.

"Bitch, don't even get me hype just yet. Where is Bella? I'll tell both y'all when we hit the lot."

"She's gonna meet us out there, but girl I got some news of my own. Did you know Janet is still messing with Mari?" I asked, walking through the café door towards Kimbella's car.

"Wait what you mean they're still messing around? I thought you *spoke* to ya man and he said they were done," she said sarcastically.

"Okay cool. Keep that sarcasm over that way. I just wanted to know if you heard it too. But it's all good, we gonna see what's up at this party. I'm good on Mari's hoe ass. Every week it's something. If it isn't when he is getting some, it's why am I tripping bout these hoes." I laughed. "It's not what I need. Y'all for real, I'm trying to get the fuck out of Greensboro. This shit is whack, and if it takes a degree, shit well I'm out. "

Kimbella stared at me intensely while she pulled from the blunt she had pre-rolled like always.

"So, are you really done, Tay? Like I don't wanna hit this party, and you be ready to dip out with his ass. He ain't shit, and I'm telling you, his lack is gonna be another man's come up. Fuck him, sis." She passed me the blunt.

"Okay cause y'all know Tana ain't with the shit's when it comes to these niggas. They all dogs, but fuck him. Let's move on. What's on the agenda for that night anyway, Tay?" she asked, accepting the blunt.

Just as I was about to answer, my phone started buzzing again, and I knew it was Omari. Looking up, I saw him about to approach the car, but an all-black Benz pulled up with deep tint. The girls and I were admiring the car when we saw Mari get in.

"Shit Tay, who the fuck does Mari's little ass know with big toys like that?" Santana asked, lighting the blunt back.

"Bitch, right. He's the same nigga who can't buy you a gift to save his life. Wait, I forgot the gifts come when you about to claw his face out." Kimbella burst out laughing with Tana in tow, choking on the weed.

"Man, fuck both of y'all. It doesn't even matter, but Tana to answer your question I told Mari I couldn't come, but we are pulling up and showing out. I need to be more social," I joked, making them both burst out laughing again.

They knew me, and that was far from my plan. I was gonna fuck shit up and then leave.

"Whatever bitch, we know you. Well, that gives us three days to find outfits and try and get Tamia to do our hair. You gotta ask Tana because she loves your ass," Bella stated.

"Well if y'all tipped like me or ever came to your appointments on time maybe she would love you too." She stuck her tongue out.

DIINNGGG DIIIINNGGG!

Just as I got my appetite, the bell rang meaning we have six minutes to get to class. Ten for me cause I needed to stop by my locker and grab my snacks. Just as I get to my locker and the girls go their own way, I see Mari turn the corner coming in my direction. I tried my best to get my locker open and close, but he was there in no time, towering over me like a palm tree. I swear this nigga was fine, but fine doesn't mean faithful and loving.

"What, Mari? I gotta get to class." I rolled my eyes, shifting from one leg to the other.

"Damn, it's like that? First, you can't support my party and then you too good to speak to me, Tay? I thought we were good wassup, yo?"

"Man, bye with that 'we good' bullshit. I'm good, nigga. You need to take that begging on to Janet's ass. That's where you lay now, baby," I said, trying to walk past him, but he grabbed my arm, pushing me into my locker just hard enough to get my attention.

"Keep trying me Octavia and I will show the fuck out." He started to squeeze my neck while kissing my lips. He then whispered, "I will see you at my party and start picking up the phone before I have to embarrass your ass. I'll hit you up till then. I'll be busy, so gone head before I get even more upset," he snarled, and I walked way holding my throat.

Hitting me was normal, but he never tried at school, so I knew it was just to send a message. Omari wanted people to respect him, and I can understand that, but I was done letting him jack me up like just anybody. Gathering my belonging out my locker, I went to my last class of the day. The last thing I needed was to be late and hear Mr. Henry's mouth about how being late will become me.

After school, I met up with Kimbella first since her class was right next to mine on E Hall. By the time we caught up to Santana, she was in a heated argument with her twin sister Soraya. They stay arguing and fighting, and we always break them up. Soraya was always feeling left out, but that's only because she's cool with Janet's thot ass, and we don't fuck with the enemy. Walking up, Kimbella spoke up first which I knew would start something because she doesn't like Raya and Raya can't stand Bella.

"What's going on, Tana?" Bella asked stepping beside Tana.

"Man, nothing. Raya is mad cause she wanna go to the party and like I told her ass, you were driving, so she has to ask you. If she ain't have so much mouth all the time, maybe it wouldn't be so hard to ask," Tana said, rolling her eyes at Raya.

"First off, I'm good. I'll ride with my people. I be damned if I jump in her piece of shit car." Raya chuckled.

Just when Tana and Bella were about to blank, Janet and her friend Kaz walk up eyeing Tana and me.

"Damn, so why we ain't get no invite? I mean damn if y'all gonna come for my girl make sure it's fair," Janet said, smiling at me.

"Bitch please, it's never fair when it's all of y'all and just me, so wassup cause y'all walked up like y'all got some business to handle," Bella said, dropping her bag ready for whatever as always.

"Damn Octavia, you need a guard dog now? Raya and Kaz, let's go. Bae just texted me, and we're good for tonight, so I gotta be ready for daddy." Janet snickered, looking at me.

Without thinking, shit like I gave a fuck, I swung and hit Janet dead in the eye. I kept swinging till I felt my hair being yanked. I looked up and saw Tana pulling Kaz off me, and Bella had Raya on the ground. Janet smacked me, and I got right back with her ass. Just when I was getting in her ass, I was lifted, and even that didn't stop me.

"Aye ma, chill out with that swinging," a deep voice said.

I looked back and didn't recognize him. I looked back for my friends, and two guys were holding them back laughing, but Tana had a focused death glare. I looked in the direction of where she was staring and saw Omari fixing up Janet and asking her if *they* are alright. Right then, I knew I was done with his trifling ass. He had fucked completely up, and there was no coming back.

"Let me GO!" I screamed at the nigga holding me back.

"Nah man, y'all are coming with us, lil lady. Omari, handle your business, and I'll hit you when I'm ready to talk. I got shorty and her girls. This ain't a good look though youngin," he said and lifted me while his boys did the same to Santana and Kimbella.

When we got to his car, I noticed it was the same Benz from earlier and that's when I got nervous. He let me inside and went to get my things. I pulled out my phone and texted Tana and Kimbella the same text, **Oh I'm DONE**, and waited for ole boy to come back.

While driving me home, I kept thinking about Mari asking if *they* were okay. He didn't even check on me, and the nigga just let me leave with this random ass nigga. The tears started to fall, and I tried to turn my body towards the window so that he wouldn't see.

"Ain't no point in hiding that ya hurt, lil lady. You gave ole girl the business all for what Omari's ass?" he asked never taking his eyes off the road.

"Can you just get me home? I don't wanna talk about it, and honestly, it isn't your concern!" I barked and again turned to my thoughts as he drove me home.

When he pulled up, I jumped out and hightailed it towards my house. Stopping in my tracks, I turned around and walked to the driver side. I bent down looking at him, and that's when I saw how sexy this nigga was. He had long ass locks that he had in two rope braids. He was wearing this all-white outfit with Red Jordan 12s, and this nigga smelled like heaven.

"Did ya forget something lil lady because I thought for a minute you were coming to finish me off." He laughed.

"No. Look, I'm sorry for how I jumped down ya throat but right now I'm in my feelings, and that harsh shit I can get from my girls. Thanks for the ride." I paused, waiting for a name.

He opened the door, and I stepped back feeling my heart jump.

"Amir," he answered with his had held out.

"Umm okay. Well, thank you, Amir." I placed my hand in his, and instead of shaking it as I was expecting, he kissed the back.

"You're welcome, Ms. Octavia." He smirked, kissed my hand again, and hopped in the car and left.

I stood there all kinds of moist and struck. He was gentle and sweet and fine as fuck, but he obviously ran with Omari, hence him knowing my name and that means he probably is the same. Shaking the thought, I went inside and showered. Both my parents would be home soon, so I pulled my phone out and texted my girls to tell them when just happened.

Chapter Two

OMARI MOORE

I can't believe Octavia would do some dumb shit like jumping on Janet. Man, I just checked her ass about the shit, and the first thing she does is fight the girl. Shit, to be honest, I don't give a fuck about her fighting Janet. I more so wanna be mad cause Janet is carrying my seed. Looking over at her I know I fucked up something good, but I don't regret my child. I was driving Janet to the doctor for an emergency checkup since she wasn't too far along.

I was heated with Janet ass too though. Like why are you fighting and starting shit with my girl knowing you pregnant? I looked back at her, and all the anger jumped out.

WAP!

"Owww, Mari! Why you hit me, and you know I'm pregnant?" she asked, holding her face.

WAP!

"Bitch, you must have got hit hard as fuck questioning my ass, and for two why the fuck you out here being reckless carrying my seed. Bitch, if you lose this baby, we gonna dead this shit."

"I didn't start shit. I told Raya and Kaz it was time to go! Next thing I know your lil play house bitch swung, so of course, I gave her what she wanted. She will know next time." She smirked.

"See that mindset that you got is gonna get you even more fucked up than what Tay did to your ass. Man, get the fuck out and go check on my seed. I need to make a call really quick," I said, pulling up at the office and taking my phone out.

Janet looked like she wanted to protest but then thought right and got the fuck out and slamming my door.

"Ungrateful bitches, man." I scoffed and dialed Tavia's number only to go straight to voicemail. I tried about five more times and then texted her.

Me: *We need to talk, yo. Stop the games.*

After about an hour Janet was coming back out, and I still hadn't spoken to Octavia. I was really getting upset, so I dropped Janet off and headed to Octavia's house. I knew her parents were home, but her mom loved me, and her dad well he ain't never stepped, so I guess he with this shit. He always looks at me like he wanna beat my ass, but he knows better. I rang the doorbell, and she came to the door.

"What, Mari? We have nothing to speak on. I need you to leave before my parents come out and call them boys, goodbye," she stated and tried to close the door, but I put my foot in the way and grabbed her arm.

"Just come take a ride with me to my crib so that we can talk man and stop all this. I don't wanna fight, and I really just want you to hear me and for me to get to hear you out."

"For what, Mari? Obviously, you chose your side, so this is pointless as fuck, and you know it." Tears started to fall, and I felt myself getting angry.

"Man, look, you can either cry all day or get these answers to your questions I know that you're asking yourself. I love you Octavia, and I wanna work this shit out. Come on."

I pulled her out to my car and helped her in. I got I on the driver side and pulled off to my apartment. Yeah, a nigga was eighteen with his own crib thanks to the streets. I wasn't running these streets yet, but my boys and I were about to be making major moves, and I needed my queen right beside me. Tay doesn't know it, but that's her. She wants to leave and go off to college right when things are about to pop off. Amir is gonna put me on soon I can feel it, and shit if he doesn't, he can be left behind.

Pulling up to my apartment, I got out and waited for Tay, but she was being stubborn as always, so I went to get her out.

"Come on, Tay. I really ain't in the mood after how you showed out today."

She jumped out and started swinging on me in the parking lot. After a few slaps on my arms, I swung and slapped the shit out of her. I grabbed her arms and pulled her towards my door and pushed her inside. Once I got in, I was met by her fist, and that bitch got a good one right in my nose. I saw my blood trickle down and hit my floor, and I was on her ass. See Tay would fight but didn't like to. We went rounds, and she always stayed, but this nah. I could tell my baby was mad, but she wasn't gonna beat my ass, and I wasn't switching shit up for her ass either. I was growing tired of this fighting and still not fucking to fix it. I swear my baby just need this dick.

She came back and hit me in my shit again, and I black out. I grabbed her by her hair, and I punched her till I felt better.

"You're a bum ass nigga, Mari. I swear I fucking hate your ass. This is why you ain't getting none. I'm done with your ass and that bitch and y'all fucking baby. You can have this shit! You fucking hear me, nigga! Your punk ass hit me and bitches all over but won't step to a nigga to save his life and thinks that grants respect!" she screamed, getting her things like she was gonna walk out after that.

"Man, see that's where you got me fucked up Tay," I said and locked the front door.

"Move, Mari. I'm not staying here for you to beat my ass. I'm done. You don't get it, huh? I'm leaving like your other ex who probably got fed up looking banged up too!" she spat, and I thought about Maya. I thought about how I loved her trifling ass, and she tried to leave me. I looked at Tay and saw she wanted the same outcome.

"Cool, you can get out just like she did, bitch!" I said calmly and walked over to Tay.

I reached behind her and pulled her hair back making her fall and hit the table. She screamed in pain, but I wasn't letting up. I pulled her back to the bedroom and tied her to my bedpost.

"Mari, what the fuck you are doing? Please just let me go." She kicked and screamed trying to get loose.

"Nah, you wanna be like Maya, remember? You wanna go out like she did. Well, you about to, Tay." I slapped and punched her till she shut up and unzipped my pants.

"Mari, this ain't you. Stop, please! You know I'm not ready. Please just stop," she begged, but that went on death ears.

I pulled my mans out and dug straight into her pussy. Man, my baby was tight as fuck. I pulled out and turned her over making her wince out in pain from the tie twisting. I spit on my dick and then her asshole. I felt her jump, and she started screaming. I fucked her long and hard till she passed out. I kept going feeling my nut rise and I came all over her face. When I was done, I took a shower, got dressed, and went to Janet's house.

The last thing I wanted was to hurt Tay, but all that shit she was talking really got to a nigga. I'm not a bitch ass nigga and won't be treated as such. I knew when she woke up she wasn't going to snitch, so I decided to go to my boy Jones' house and chill till I figured out my moves.

Chapter Three

OCTAVIA

I woke up in the most pain I had ever felt in my life. I hurt all over, and I didn't think I could move. I took all the strength I had left and go up and staggered to the bathroom. Looking at my face, I burst out into tears screaming and yelling. How could he do this to me for him fucking up? Why didn't I just walk away like usual? I sat there and cried my eyes out till I couldn't cry anymore.

Jumping in his shower, I washed up and put some of his clothes on and searched for my phone and purse. Looking around, I found my phone shattered and all my money gone. Shaking my head, I opened the door and walked home. Pissed and hot I thought of what I would say to my parents when I got home. Here I was walking from W. Market Street all the way to E. Market because my nigga beat and raped me, and I was trying to figure out a cover story at maybe three a.m.

Just as I was about to cross over Spring Garden, a red Lambo pulls up and greets me on the other side. Scared and nervous I kept staggering, I didn't have time for nobody else's bullshit, and I would fight before they just took my ass. The windows rolled down and here was this fine ass nigga Amir, looking like I had pissed him off.

"Fuck you looking like that for, and why in the fuck are you walking from Mari's crib like he doesn't have wheels?" He glared at me.

"Look, we got into it, and I hit him. So, of course, any nigga would swing back. I'm good, so you can go now," I stated flatly and kept going. He pulled into the shopping center parking lot, got out, and walked up to me.

"Why are you covering for this nigga, Octavia? He ain't worth shit if he's gotta hit you to get his point across. Even if you hit him, no real man is going to swing back," he said thoughtfully. Considering both my eyes were beginning to turn black, I could tell he was interested. I was melting, and he didn't even know it.

"Can you please just take me home, Amir?" I burst into tears, and he grabbed me and carried me to his car. The inside had black and red leather interior with a Bluetooth radio that looked like it played DVDs too.

The ride back to my house was a quiet one, and he never looked at me. I kept stealing glances at him wondering if he was different or just trying to make me feel better. Just when I was about to speak, his phone went off, and when he looked and ignored it, I knew it had to be his girl. Rolling my eyes, I sat back and went back to my thoughts on what to tell my parents. I figured I would tell them I got jumped by some girls while I was at the store, and I broke up with Mari, so that's why I walked.

"Can you drop me off a few blocks off and I'll walk from there? I don't need Mari seeing me with you and think I'm fucking you," I said just above a whisper.

"Nah, I can take you home though, lil lady."

"I don't wanna be the cause of y'all beef though, Amir. Obviously, you work for Mari and his boys, so I hate for you to get cut out helping me," I said as nice as I could.

"Look, let me worry about Mari. He won't be a problem for you anymore. Here, this is my phone. I noticed you weren't on yours the whole ride so you must not have it, but lock your number in and I'll give you a call, okay?" he said, looking deep into my eyes. I couldn't even speak back because I had gotten stuck inside his. "You hear me, lil lady?"

"Uh yeah, but actually my phone is broken so give me yours, and I'll hit you when I get mine," I said not intending on ever calling this man. This was too much drama already.

"Check this. I'll be back okay. Go take care of yourself. Give me a minute, and I'll be by to check on you, iight?" he asked, smiling and showing all his pearly whites.

"Yeah, iight," I said as I got out and went inside.

As soon as my mom saw me, I told her the story, and she called my dad. I told them I was okay, and I just needed to rest, so they let me go to my room. I knew this wasn't over, but for now, it was just fine with me.

Chapter Four

SORAYA LEE

Here I am minding my own business at my girl Kaz's house and who do I see pull up at Octavia's house but Amir Montee. Seeing him at Tay's house had me upset because I had been trying to get at this nigga for the longest. I had just sucked the skin off his dick three hours ago and couldn't get fucked by him to save my life. Now I see why he had been ignoring my calls all day. Taking a few snaps, I sent them straight to Janet, who I knew would tell Mari. Shit, by the way Tay got out looking, Mari had already beat her ass.

Oh, it was no secret that Omari hit his girls. Tay was green to that when she first got with him. Janet tells us how he beats Tay's ass and comes to her house to fuck his frustration off. She claims he doesn't hit her, but she damn sure had a red mark on her face when I Face Timed her ass earlier.

What I didn't understand was what Amir saw in that fat bitch anyways. She never straightened that nappy ass natural hair. Her shit was just everywhere, she was fat as fuck, and ate all the time. Like the bitch's locker is full of snacks. Her, my sister, and they ugly ass black ass friend Kimbella had it coming. See Kimbella doesn't like me because I fucked her ole boy a few times, and he still pays my way. She knows we are fucking, and that's why she stays up my kitty kat.

Most niggas want me because I was light skin and thick. See Santana was my twin, but she was more so black than she was Asian. I got all my mommy face and some black woman's body I swear because I kept niggas drooling. My curly, jet black, silky hair bounced down my back as I waited for Kaz to come out with the weed so that we could smoke. I pulled out my phone and called Amir.

"Man, what yo?" he answered.

"Damn, you weren't like this a few hours ago. What did I do, daddy?" I purred.

"Raya, what do you want. I'm busy, and I got shit to do. A few hours ago your mouth was occupied with my dick so of course I wasn't fazed. You weren't yapping then either. Now, what's up 'for I bang this shit on ya?"

"I just wanted to see you, but obviously you busy. When are you gonna come give me what I need though?" I smiled, putting him on speaker just as Kaz came. Putting my finger to my mouth, I told her to listen while I smiled ear to ear. Yeah, this was MY nigga.

BEEP! BEEP!

Looking at my phone, I could see this nigga had hung up dead on my ass. Kaz burst out laughing at my ass as I put my phone down and started to roll.

"Bitch, shut up! Daddy was just busy getting me a surprise. Where's yo nigga though?" I asked, laughing back.

"Girl, don't worry about Kaziah she gets hers, but I'm not after no other bitch's man. I got my own, hoe." She stuck her tongue out and passed me the grinder.

I looked up just in time to see his red Lambo coming down the street again. I started smiling ear to ear as he got closer and slowed down. When I saw this nigga pass me and pull into Octavia's driveway this time, I was livid. He got out with a few bags from the mall and what looked like a Verizon wireless bag. I snapped him knocking and being let in by Octavia's dad.

"Well bitch, I guess he y'all nigga now. You just like Janet, huh?" Kaziah burst out laughing.

"Yeah, we will see, lil bitty."

I rolled my eyes and called Amir again and again just to get the voicemail. I lit the blunt and just watched as he came out with Tay, and they spoke. When they were done, he kissed her cheek, and she hugged him, and he sped off.

Shit, me being me I called Janet to see if Mari was there. I was gonna get my nigga by any means. Octavia should have stayed in her lane because Amir is more than spoked for, but she will have to find that out for herself.

After a few rings later, Janet finally picks up.

"Hey, Raya. Wassup bihh?" Janet answered sounded excited.

"Nothing girl, I'm still at Kaz's house. Are you chilling with ya baby daddy? I got more info," I said, getting to the point.

"Damn bitch, you can't even ask about your niece or nephew?" she scoffed and passed Mari the phone.

"Wassup?" he answered.

"Aye, I'm about to send some pictures of ya girl all over yo boy, Amir. I thought my bro should know how the bitch really gets down." I smiled.

"Yeah, send me that. I'm out." *BEEP, BEEP!* And with that, he was gone, and I sent the pictures.

I don't care how anybody feels about what I'd just done. Shit, Amir was for me, so if he is buying shit, it must mean she is fucking with him hard. Amir is very established in the game, and one day he's gonna make me his queen, and Tay is just gonna have to find someone new. I done fought more bitches than can count because they thought he would leave me alone, but nah, I got it just like that. He gets mad and leaves me alone for a little while, but he always hit my line when he needs me most.

Gathering my things, I tell Kaz I'm leaving and start walking towards Avalon Trace Apartments where Tana and I lived with our mom. She was a beautiful woman, and nobody liked her either. Shit, Tana doesn't even like our own mother, but that's just because she is a daddy's girl. Everybody says I'm just like mommy, and I believe it. Hell, I wanna look that good at Thirty-five years old.

Walking in the door, my mommy was sitting on the couch smoking a Newport and watching *Love & Hip Hop.* She swore she could still pull niggas like them with her old ass, and to be honest my mommy just might be able to. Her Asian skin was blemish free, and her silky, long jet-black hair was bone straight on its own.

"Hey mommy, you cooked? It smells good in here," I asked, putting my stuff on the table.

"Nah, that yo sista in there. What you got in yo bag girl?" she asked with her accent strong as fuck.

"Oh, I guess I'll starve. I don't trust the hoe, and I got you an eighth from Scooby's ass. They say it's some fire, Ma." I handed her the bag and cigars.

"Nah Bev, said it's fye, so that's what it is. Look, my friend coming over so y'all gotta go. I don't need y'all in my business. Do ya hear me, Santana?"

"Yeah Ma, I'm already gone," Tana said, pushing past me walking towards our room.

"Damn, excuse you. Why you gotta an attitude?" I laughed.

"Nah, Raya. It's not the time, so move before you get more than you can take," she said, sizing me up. I knew I was no match for my sister, and I hated to fuck up my face.

"Look, I didn't know she was gonna start no shit, Tana. You gotta believe me."

"No Raya, what I know is you took them bitches' side a long time ago. I know you knew she was fucking Octavia's man, and you had to know she was pregnant. That's what I know, now move so that I can go." She pushed past me again, walking out the door not even saying bye to mommy.

See, disrespectful shit like that gets under my skin. I know mommy likes me better cause Tana looks and acts like our dad. More than likely she going to his house anyways— good riddance. I packed me an overnight bag and went through Bingham Park to get to Kaz's house. My mommy says she's gotta boo, but we never get to meet him. It was more than likely because he was somebody else's husband or man in general.

Getting to Kaz's house, I knocked, and her dad came and let me in. I hated when he was here, but loved it all the same. I dropped my bag and sat on the couch. After closing the door, he came and sat across from me. Sitting up to show my full breasts, I stared him down as he did me.

"So, where's Kaz, Mr. Williams?" I smirked, swinging my leg.

"She should be back in about an hour. She went to them fish tables for me." He smiled and walked towards me.

"So, we have about forty-five minutes, huh?"

"Yeah, give or take. Let's go to the guest bedroom, Raya. I need this today right now," he said and slid his hands into my loose pajama shorts.

I moaned out in pleasure begging him not to stop because I needed this nut just as bad. He used his free hand to tickle my nipple, so I leaned back and pulled my shirt up. When he stops, I look at him crazy cause I was so close.

Picking me up, he went to the guest bedroom and started to undress. Now Mr. Williams wasn't the fittest man, but he kept himself up, and he was so damn fine. His scar on his face scared the shit out of me but turned me on at the same.

Doing the same, I teased him coming out of my clothes, and then I turned and pushed him on the bed. I straddled his hard dick and slid down slow making sure to squeeze my muscles driving him crazy. I rode him all the way to the glory, and we were both dead tired. When I was done, I laid down only for him to grab my legs and bury his face inside my pussy.

I arched my back as he ate my pussy till I came and didn't stop. He kept going until I went limp and passed out. When I woke up, Kaz still wasn't home, so we showered and went back into the living room to watch a movie. Mr. Williams went and got my money as he always did and brought Chinese food back with him. Oh yeah, this good pussy ain't free. I smashed and waited for Kaz, but was thinking about how to get back in good with Amir. That's where the real money was, and I was gonna get all of it. This was the last time I settled for less. That's when it clicked. I knew how to get Amir in my web, and it will be easy as fuck.

Chapter Five

SANTANA LEE

I was fed up with my momma and my sister, and I was ready to leave with Tay to head to Charlotte for school. We only have the weekend in our way, and then we graduate. Turning onto Tay's street, I walked past Kaz's house. When I saw her walking towards the railroad tracks, I knew she was up to no good. I knocked on Tay's door, and Mr. Jones opened the door looking like he was about to head out himself.

"Hey, Santana. Octavia is in her room," he said swiftly leaving out.

"Uh, okay!" I yelled and went to find Tay.

"Ummm bitch, I know Janet didn't do that much damage because you were whooping her ass!" I yelled, walking up on my girl's bruised and battered face. The shit had Mari all over it. Just as I was about to blank, she burst into tears.

"He took it, Tana. He took my only possession, yo. He took that shit when it was gonna be his anyway," she sobbed.

"Man, no Tay. He knew he didn't deserve it, so that's why he took it. Aww baby girl, talk to me. What happened?" I asked, taking the weed out my bag and grinding it down.

"He came by wanting to talk, but I was like nah. But, he put me in his car, and we went to his place. I started swinging because I thought about his helping Janet's bitch ass instead of me and him checking on me after being there for her first. Bitch, I just lost it, and we got to fighting in the house. He got me good, and the next thing I know..." She paused as more tears fell. "He was inside me and didn't even care I was screaming," she cried.

This shit hurt me more than she knew. I couldn't stand Omari at first, but now I have pure hate for that nigga, and he was gonna get his.

"So how did you get home, and I know you went to the police, right Tay?"

"No, because I plan on taking care of the situation. He isn't getting away this time," she said in a cold tone that I've never heard her use. Mari done woke up a beast and don't even know it.

"Well, I got you when you need me, but again how did you get home?" I asked.

"Girl, that's the crazy part. I was walking down W. Market on the way here since my phone was shattered, and I didn't bring any cash to get a ride. So, I get to Spring Garden and guess who pulls the fuck up?" She beamed.

"Bitch, spit it out!"

"Amir," she said and smiled hard as fuck.

"Okay, so then what? I mean damn he saw you like this, and doesn't he work for Mari?" I asked, seeing how dramatic things could get.

"Well, he took me home, and we talked, but not much cause his phone kept ringing meaning he's gotta girl somewhere. He did bring me a few outfits and a phone." She pointed to the unopened bags on the desk.

"Damn, he did all this, and you think he's gotta whole woman at home? Bitch, did you even see these price tags or these clothes?"

I held up a candy red, mini dress that was one sleeved and sheer red at the top. Grabbing the other bags, I was too through. This man went all out for my girl, and if he does have a girl, her days might be numbered the way he showed out.

"I plan on giving him this stuff back. I get paid next week, so I'll give him the phone too. Girl, he's so fucking sexy, and he smells so fucking good. When he spoke to me, it felt like he looked into my soul, and I swear girl I thought a bitch had floated." She laughed, holding her stomach and wincing in pain.

"I feel you. It kind of makes you feel like you're helping him cheat, but are you sure he is taken, Tay? Like did he speak to his girl right in front of you?" I asked.

"I mean no, but he would sneak to look at the phone when it rang and then look at me while ignoring it. Why else would a nigga do that, Tana?"

"True, damn that sucks. Well, his boy has been trying my ass too. You know I ain't biting though, I got plans girl," I said, thinking about Trez.

When we got into the fight, he was holding me back spitting game the whole time. Somehow this nigga got my number and texted me as soon as I woke up this morning. Trez was cute as fuck, but I don't do the whole thug thing. I wanted to go to school, get a career, get married, have some babies, and be happy. That lifestyle can't bring me that.

"So, what you gonna do, Tana? You are still pure baby, so you can adventure a little," Tay said, bringing me out my thoughts, "You aren't like your mom and Raya. You got dreams. Trez might seem like a thug, but you would be surprised how many thugs give the game up for the one," she said, smirking.

I put all the clothes in their bags and got into bed with my best friend. I didn't want to think about Trez. I just wanted to make sure my best friend was okay. Looking at her still smiling scared me because Tay was my heart, and I don't know how I will act when I am face to face with Mari.

We laid there talking and chilling until around seven o'clock when Bella got there in her jammies with movies and snacks in tow. When we needed each other, we knew how to be there. One thing is for sure Raya and Janet are gonna get theirs and Kaz too. Mari, well, his days are numbered.

While Bella did Tay's hair, since Janet's only defense was hair pulling, my mind wondered off to Trez again. I never dated anyone, but not because I was ugly because I was far from it. Yeah, I didn't get the light, bright skin color like Soraya, but I loved my mocha brown skin. I was the skinny one of the bunch as they say, but I just knew I was thick, and I would argue Tay down that I would get there. Like always she would say that the right man would thicken me right up. Giggling, I wondered if Trez has the thick potion.

"What's so funny, bitch?" Bella asked, braiding Tay hair up.

"Girl, I'm just thinking about giving Trez a chance after playing back a little," I answered honestly.

"Yessssssss booooo! I'm excited! I think it will be a good thing for you if he can handle that mouth." Octavia laughed.

"What mouth? I am an angel. Y'all are the demon seeds over there fighting at school and shit!" I threw Tay's scarf at her.

"First off the bitch had it coming," Tay said.

"And the other two needed a warning," Bella said, high fiving Tay.

I shook my head I loved my girls, but these bitches crazy.

"Soooo about graduation; are you going tomorrow?" I asked Tay since she still had bruising on her face.

"Oh, I will be walking that stage. Mari's gonna be there, and I want him to know he didn't break me at all. I also plan on being at that party. I need a new boo thang, and he might be there."

"Bitch, I doubt it," Bella joked.

"Shit, you're right my standards are up there."

"I don't know Tay he might just be there. Doesn't Amir work for Mari?" I asked again since she went past it earlier.

"Amir, wait what? Did he helped this nigga or something?" Bella asked.

"No, he helped Tay. That's how this hoe got home and them clothes on the desk you asked about when you walked in. He also bought her a phone, but Tay thinks he's taken, and he just might be."

"Damn Santana, I got this. I can tell my story." She laughed. "And he does have a girl Bella, ain't no might. Enough about Amir, what do y'all think about the party?"

"I'm down," Bella agreed.

"Yeah, me too bihh, for whatever. You gonna wear this though," I said, holding up the red dress with matching pumps.

"Oooouuuu yes Tay, I see it, and when I am done with your

makeup, you will be flawless," Bella said, finishing the last braid and putting it into a bun.

"Thanks y'all for being here. Now, all I need now is a drink and a blunt, and I don't even drink," Tay said. And with that, she went and wrapped up her hair and jumped in the shower.

I hated that she was going through this, and I was ready to handle Mari and get past this. I let Bella curl my hair, and we all went to bed. Tomorrow we all have to just get past work then it's pamper time to get ready for graduation.

We had already got our appointments set for Tamia at six o'clock tomorrow, and I swear if these bitches make me late, I will disown them at the shop. Tamia is my dad's new girlfriend and the dopest hair stylist in Greensboro. Even though she is in NC right now, she has worked with people from all over and is also a celebrity stylist. The only reason she loves me as much as she does is that I'm just as nice back. I love her for my daddy Mike, and I also love being with them and their two-year-old Maddison.

See my mommy got caught cheating on my father with various men and instead of saying sorry and them working on it, she blamed him and me for why she had to. Him for always working and not making time for her, and me for being born after Raya and giving her the body she has now. It never made any sense but the woman stuck to it, and I just kept my distance. With Tamia is was always different. She and my dad have been dating for five years, and I hope he plans to tie the knot soon cause like I always told her, she would then become my mother and wouldn't have to pretend.

The strain my father is now having with me is why I will not move in with him, and I think he just doesn't see things my way. Tamia gets it, and I've told him plenty of times that I loved being here for Octavia. She was my little sister, and we were all we had. My father had money and a huge house, and to him, that was better than Creek Ridge and all the drama around there. I loved my dad, and I promised him if I ever changed my mind I would come running, and after I graduate, I'll be moving my things to his house for the summer, and then to Charlotte for school.

My mother thought she would treat me like crap forever, and she had me fucked up. After eighteen years of not eating some nights, getting beat till I bled because I had something that Soraya wanted, and for every evil name and thing said to me, I would be gone for good. I was leaving Raya and Mae to rot in the hoe ass lifestyle they are begging for. I pray every day that they get their lives right and for me be able to forgive once they do.

Rolling over, I went to bed ready to get tomorrow's day of work over with already. Better things were coming.

Chapter Six

OCTAVIA

Graduation was finally over, and the girls and I were standing side by side as our families took our pictures. I couldn't be any more happier than I currently was because I did this on my own. I pride myself on being educated, and when I have babies, I hope they take their education just as serious.

It was awkward with all our parents around. Although Tamia slayed the girl's hair, she sat back admiring her work. Mae had the nerve to side-eye her every chance she got, and I could tell Mr. Mike was getting aggravated with her. Soraya was pushed into a few pictures thanks to Mae wanting a few of her, but we all agreed to crop her out ASAP.

Maddison ran up to Santana and me asking to be in the pictures, so we both picked her up ready to pose. This girl was energetic and was hitting her own poses.

"Ahh hell no Mike, get that thing out of my kids picture. Them my babies not her, she belongs to that," Mae said, pointing to Tamia and grabbing Maddison by the arm.

"Bitch, you better get your hand off my baby before I knock your ass back to Korea where you came from. Mike, get cho baby momma cause in 2.5 I will feel defensive." Tamia jumped up and was snatching Mae's hand off a crying Madison.

"Mae move before I fuck you up out here. This day about our girls and you still on some you shit. How about your hoe ass move and find a nigga to jump on?" Mike grabbed Mae.

"Nigga, you just mad cause I won't fuck you anymore. Yeah Tamika, ya man still likes this Asian pussy. Ha, fuck me up. No nigga don't get fucked up. Girls let's go." Mae yanked back and walked off.

"Ma, I'm going with my daddy. Y'all gone head, I'm good," Tana said, stepping beside Mike and Tamia.

"Oh, so this bitch combs your nappy ass hair, and now she's your mommy. You are taking them bitches side, Tana?"

"Yeah Ma, it's like that, and don't disrespect her. Don't worry I'll have my things moved out tonight," Tana said and walked away with tears in her eyes.

"That's fine you little black bitch, I ain't want you no way. Shit, you were just the extra for my meal ticket. I'll always be straight. Soraya, let's go," Mae said. "And Tana you ain't got shit that's my house. Make your new mommy buy you what you need and see how soon they get tired of your skinny, lazy black ass," she added and sped off.

Santana stopped crying and wiped her tears just as Maddison walked up to her and hugged her.

"You hurt, Tana? Huh? You okay, Tana?" Maddison asked.

"Yeah Maddie, Tana is better than okay. How about we go talk mommy and daddy into taking us out to eat huh, then I'll be your best friend," Tana offered

"My best friend? Ooouuu!" Maddison cooed. "Mommy, I'm hungry. I hungry, mommy!" she whined and turned to wink at Tana and me. We laughed and winked back, that girl was something else.

After going to the Cheesecake Factory and then to Cold Stones for ice cream, we were tired but ready to show out for this party. We had seen Mari at graduation and decided to make him think I was cool, and I forgave him. It's crazy how he believed the whole thing. When I plan on looking single as fuck in his shit on his day, payback would be served.

Getting home, I called Tana and then Bella, and they agreed to pull up at the party around midnight since neither really wanted to stay. I decided to jump in the shower letting the hot water massage my body. Washing every part of my body, I still felt sore vaginally and anally but not so much it affects my walk. After showering, I looked over my body in my body size bathroom mirror. For a size eighteen, I was cute as hell, and I don't mean in a feeling myself kind of way, but I was genuinely beautiful.

Putting on the dress that Amir bought me and then the shoes, my mind drifted off to him and what he could be doing. He had been texting me all day and last night at work, but I didn't have time to respond, and I figured that was for the better. The last thing I needed was drama from his girl for simply holding a conversation. As a female, I would feel the same for a new female friend. Admiring myself again, I heard my phone buzz and saw that Bella and Tana were both here. Grabbing my clutch, I headed towards my parent's room and heard light weeping.

Opening their room door, I saw my mother going through my dad's phone while he showered. I knew this couldn't be good, but I had other things to handle, and I couldn't take any more negative thoughts, so I eased back and knocked.

"Come in, Tay. Your dad is in the shower. Well, look at you. Where did you get that beautiful dress? That cute boy with them locs, huh?" She smiled weakly.

"Uhh yeah Ma, but it's nothing. We are not dating or anything, and I just came to say I was leaving with Tana and Bella. Did you need me for anything before I leave, mommy?" I asked, hoping she would be honest with me.

She paused and smiled looking at me like she was the proudest woman on earth. "No, baby. You be safe and have fun. You ain't grown Tay, so don't play tonight. Let me know if you're not coming back and make sure I know where you are. I love you, have fun," she said, and I heard the shower cut off. "Go ahead before he sees that. He might kill us both." She laughed weakly again.

"Thank you, mommy. I love, you too." I kissed her cheek and sped out the house only to see a blue Malibu sitting outside. I was worried so started to call Tana to see where they were, then the window slowly went down.

"Bitch, you scared *ha-ha.* Come on. This is my new baby thanks to mommy and daddy!" Tana yelled.

"Ooouuu I see you, bitch!" I jumped in and right in time to hit the blunt.

"That's all you, Tay. We smoked already." Bella giggled.

"Bitch, you stay geeked man. Let's get this night started y'all," I said, pushing what I had just seen to the back of my mind for now.

We headed west towards Mari's apartment. I started feeling nauseous and nervous since this was where he attacked me. Then I got pissed cause it's like he didn't even care that he did this to me. The nigga rapes me and two days later is throwing a party in the same spot. This nigga didn't give a fuck.

"You good, Tay?" Tana asked as she and Bella looked back at me as we parked.

"Yeah, let's go. I'm Gucci."

"Well, let's fuck it up then bitches!" Bella yelled, twerking in the seat.

We got out and walked up looking like true bad bitches. The niggas were on us like dogs on a cat, and I was feeling the thirst. When we first walked in it was thick, so we got to our spot and checked out the scene. After about twenty minutes "Wait a Minute remix" by Phresher and Remy Ma came on, and me and my bitches started to twerk. Niggas were all over us, and we killed that shit. Out of nowhere, I felt someone grab me, and I twerked my ass silly. I knew this nigga wouldn't be able to take it, but surprisingly he was holding it down. When the song went off, I turned around and was face to face with Amir.

"Damn, you ain't happy to see a nigga, are you?" he asked, smiling.

I was so scared that I was ready to run, and I must have tried because he stopped me and just looked at me. I looked around, and Tana was smiling while Bella was looking worried and pointed. I looked in that direction, and Omari was watching me intensely with Janet on his lap. I knew he was mad, but he had no reason. I wasn't entertaining Amir, and if I was, I wasn't his girl anymore.

"No, it's not like that at all. Thanks for the dance, I gotta go." I pulled away and went outside.

Standing outside, I walked to Tana's car and was texting her to let her know I stepped outside. When I got to the car, I turned to lean back on her car and was met by a fist.

Wham!

"Bitch, you love making me look stupid, don't you?" Mari said, standing in my face.

"Mari, we not together and therefore you don't need to check me. All I did was dance, and he came and danced with me. Why you got that bitch all over you, and you over here on my case?" I asked, getting pissed.

He raised his hand as if he was going to hit me again, and then I heard him grunt.

"Oh shit!" he grunted again.

"Nigga, you don't raise your hand to no woman, you understand me?" Amir said, holding Omari in an arm lock. "Aye, lil lady come here," he said.

"No, my girl is coming. I just need to go home now," I said, holding my face and looking for Tana.

"Nah, she sent me, and I'm here, so come here," he said, letting Omari go and walking towards me. Two goons came and got Omari and took him back to the house. I was sitting there struck and unable to move. He wrapped his arms around me and then asked, "You good?"

"I'm fine Amir really thank you again, but I gotta get out of here now."

"Well, let's go. You're in good hands ma, I promise."

As much as I wanted to say no, I looked up and saw Tana talking to Trez and Bella beside her talking to the guy I know as Zoe. Both rock with Amir, but I know Zoe from around the way. He's cool as fuck just an asshole.

Getting into his car, I texted my mom letting her know I was going to get some food. We rode in silence until he finally stopped at a light and spoke. "Instead of worry about that pussy nigga, you should be focused on the real right here."

"Actually, I wasn't thinking about either. I was thinking about my mom and dad," I turned and said. "I think my parents are having issues and I don't know about going to school with them having issues," I stated honestly. I would hate to go away, and they split without talking to me. My parents always seemed so happy. I don't know what went wrong or if I was dreaming the whole time.

"Damn, I'm sorry to hear that lil lady, but my parents have been divorced for two years, and they have been at their happiest," he mentioned smiling. "What if they take the steps and being without each other brings them together?"

"I mean I never thought about it like that, to be honest, but I always believed when things get tough to hold it down together not apart because anything can happen," I said, staring him into his eyes. The way he stared back made me feel like he understood where I was coming from.

I looked away quickly and noticed that we were pulling up at the new Cook-Out on W. Wendover Avenue. I hadn't taken time to hit this one yet but wanted to for a while just to sit and eat my food fresh. He pulled into a spot, and we walked into the restaurant. After I ordered a barbecue chicken tray, no pickles, with hush puppies and fries and a tea, Amir got a double burger with mayo, lettuce, chili and slaw with double Cajun fries, and a Cheerwine.

We get our food, and he never said a word to me, so I stayed to myself. I went and found a booth while he grabbed our food. I didn't understand why he had me here and what he wanted with me. Ironically, his phone hadn't made a sound since I got in his car.

"So, you plan to stay home instead of going to school? What's the school and major if you don't mind me asking?" he asked with a mouth full of food.

"Well nasty I got accepted to UNC Charlotte with Santana, the girl you got Trez with." I giggled. "But if they don't make things work I have to be here for them both." I finished.

"I feel that well what is your major?"

"I was thinking of going for social work. I plan on having my own battered and homeless shelters, a chain of them, and I want to help women and children."

"That's what's up. You got ambition."

"What about you? What do you do for a living?"

"I own a few properties, and I do a little here and there to make it. You not too green so don't even come at me like that, lil lady. This here is me getting to know you. You have time to get to know me." He smiled again.

"Well, I have one more question, and I am done."

He looked at me and then sat back in the booth. "Shoot."

"Do you have a girl?"

"Damn, you outspoken, huh? No, I don't have a girl, and I don't keep girls. I want a woman. Someone to have my children, cook banging ass meals and help me grow to be the best I can be. I need a female to grow with me, so I don't need her to be perfect. I need her to love me," he said, and I took in what he was saying.

"So, with all the girls out here why aren't you taken?"

"Man, these bitches only see my money and nice shit. Can't one female tell you info about my crib, my family, or my life. They hear my name and have nothing but stories to tell man." He ate a fry and shook his head.

"So, it ain't true? You're not this stone-cold nigga?" I asked, getting nervous as fuck because lord knows I didn't have any business with this man.

"Nah don't tell yourself that, cause when someone messes with something that belongs to me, I can be really cold," he said in a tone that made my pussy jump.

It was getting late, and we were cruising on the highway. I had already told my mom that I was at Bella's house and told the girls I'd keep them posted but that I was good. Amir had 97.5 playing smooth R&B, and I was enjoying the ride. We got off on exit that looked like the middle of nowhere. Taking out my phone, I turned 'Find My iPhone' on and texted the girls to stay on it.

We drove down a dark secluded road for about five miles, and I could only see maybe two houses from the highway. We pulled up to a large gate, and he spoke into the intercom. The gates opened and we drove in. My mouth dropped when I saw his mansion. Hell, I might as well say estate because Amir had two guest houses that looked like they had maybe five bedrooms minimum. When he finally parked in front of the stairs, I turned and looked at him like he was crazy.

"Amir, why am I here? You know we can't be like that. I just got rid of Mari's ass. On top of the fact that you just said you don't bring girls to ya house."

He just laughed and got out the car like I had just told the joke of the century. I watched as he walked around to the fifth step and turned and looked back. I gave him a look like he had me fucked up because I still don't know Amir.

"Come on. I told you I don't bite, and I ain't into that forceful shit unless asked." He smirked and licked his lips, making me giggle a little. "Just come chill. It's been a minute since I was able to just chill and I wanna relax. Come on, Octavia," he said, and the way my name rolled out his mouth, I couldn't feel my legs, but they were helping themselves out his car.

"Iight, but I can't stay the night Amir, so don't play when I say I'm ready to go then it's go time, you got me?" I sashayed past him and waited by the door. I knew he was probably looking at my ass, but I wanted to see the inside of the house.

"You and that mouth of yours gonna get you hemmed up, keep on." He chuckled, opening the door and letting me inside first. "Whatcha think? It's chill type of place, right?"

Chill my ass; this was family play dates, baby shower, and a birthday party type of place. He had all white furniture with gold tables and bookcases. His kitchen was built for a chef, and his backyard was huge with two pools. He took me room to room and then his office, which was also a library. I walked around looking at the books and the authors making mental notes to check a few out.

"What you know about half these authors , boy? Most niggas don't like to read. They like math better. You know what I mean?" I asked, looking at a Mz. Lady P book he had that I had been trying to find.

"This room is actually for my sister. When she is going through something or just wants to get away, I let her come here and read. I mean she done read these a billion and one times, but for some reason, she reads based off what she is going through. She is a bookworm, but

I love her," he said, showing me a picture. She was young and beautiful. They looked like twins which was crazy.

"I love to read too so I know I would love her. But this book is one that I have wanted to read since she dropped it. You think she would mind me taking this home? I'll give it back." I poked my lip out and hugged to the book like Maddison would.

"Damn, you trying to get spoiled already, huh?" He smiled. "You good go ahead, I'm about to turn a movie on, you coming?"

"Yeah."

And with that, I followed him all the way back downstairs to his entertainment room, the whole time wondering why he was single. Here he was charming yet demanding. I enjoyed his company and his conversation, sitting beside him on the couch as he browsed Netflix and found a movie.

For the remainder of the night, we chilled, watched movies, and talked just like he said we would. I found out that he was twenty-four and had no children, and was from South Carolina. He didn't really like going out and clubbing unless it was business or he had a legit reason to be out. I liked that because I was a homebody myself.

❧

When I looked at my phone, it was five in the morning, and I was finally getting tired. "Amir, I need to be getting to Bella's house," I said, shaking him because he fell asleep on *Trolls*.

"Damn, what time is it?" he asked, looking on the TV then jumping up. "Look, I gotta take care of something. So why don't you chill here, and I'll take you back when I get back."

I was hesitant, and he must have been able to tell because he walked up to me and kissed me long and hard. Closing my eyes and my legs, I felt my whole body catch on fire. The way his lips felt pressed against mine, the way his tongue massaged mine like he needed to taste me. He started to rub my nipples, and I moved his hand.

"I'm sorry Amir, I can't. It's just I haven't been with anyone, and I need some time, plus we just met. I do like you, but like I said we just met."

"I understand. Don't sweat it. Look, how about I take you to your girl's crib, and I'll pick y'all up and we all chill. What you think?" he asked, helping me off the couch and fixing my clothes.

"I'll ask when I get there and see where their heads are at I guess." I smiled.

He pulled me in for another kiss and said, "You know you mine now Octavia, right? I don't play about mine." His tone was cold but loving. I was his, and I liked the sound of that.

"I'm yours, Amir. Now take come on before I disappoint you again." I giggled.

"I'm never disappointed. It will be mine too soon enough. I'll wait as long as I need, love," he said, and with that, he took me to Bella's and was gone.

I don't know if me being with him so soon was the right thing, and I was already thinking twice. Knocking on the door, I decided I would text him and let him know that maybe we were making a mistake. I would let him know how much I enjoyed my night with him, but it was the last. I had other things I had to worry about.

Chapter Seven

AMIR MONTEE JR

J umping on the highway, I was ready to get down to business and get this money. I had called a meeting after leaving with Octavia at the party, and I wanted to address this shit head on before niggas had time to think twice. Omari had me fucked up. Here he was trying to get me to work with him and make a name for himself while working sloppily.

I was fed up trying to show this lil nigga how to move and to be honest my gut had been telling me this nigga was weak and needed to be let loose. I made sure Trez and Bleek were already there because I didn't need any issues tonight. After getting confirmation that they plus them niggas were there, I pulled up and lit my blunt. I wanted to be calm when I talked business.

Stepping inside the warehouse, everybody stood up and nodded as I walked by. I dapped up Bleek then Trez and looked around for the crew that I was here for.

"Iight niggas, I won't keep y'all long because I know we got plays to make, so this won't take me long at all. Omari, y'all cut. If I see anybody helping or assisting these niggas, you will be dealt with. If y'all niggas try and step, we are here. This is my turf Mari, and you seemed to have forgotten that. This also means you done with Octavia. She's good on you my G," I said, looking him dead in the eyes. I don't need him getting anything mixed up.

"What you mean we cut though, Amir?" he said venom all in his voice. Bleek stood up, and I pulled him back. Walking up to Mari, I burst out laughing.

"Oh, so my seed going hungry is funny, huh? I thought we were good, and as far as Tay she's broken in my nigga, so you can have her." He chuckled, dapping his homeboy Bryant up.

WHAP, WHAP, WHAP!

"Now get that nigga up out of here and y'all get back to ya post. We are done. Bleek and Trez, let me speak with y'all really quick," I said.

After dropping Mari on his ass, his boys helped him up and dipped. I didn't have time for words cause they cost ya. I sent my message, so if he wants smoke, he knows how to get my attention.

"Wassup pretty boy, whatcha need?" Bleek asked, lighting his blunt and sitting in a chair in my office. Bleek has been down since grade school. My nigga was with me when I first started with my dad. We both done seen and did a lot, and he never switched up and never complained.

"Shut cho ugly ass up. Aye Trez, get out cho phone and give me what I need nigga," I said, talking about our next pick up.

"Man pops is talking about next week instead of the week after that. I told him you didn't need it, but the old guy said it's a gift," he said, looking like he didn't understand.

"Cool. Nah, next week works. It's the night out this way with nothing but the boys patrolling, so I don't need them in my shit. So, about this Mari situation what y'all think?"

"He doesn't want this shit, man. He's just mad you took his girl. Shit, after the party nigga was talking mad shit. How do you think he walked in with that black eye, not in front of me, nigga." Bleek hit his chest like King Kong. "Shit, if this nigga wasn't all over Santana's ass maybe we could have left and handled his ass."

"Nah, he's a lil nigga. He don't want these problems, and Trez wassup with you and lil Tana?"

"Man, baby girl is bad as fuck, but she be playing and acting like she doesn't want my ass. The way she's been texting me, I know she wants me, bruh." Trez said. "But she did say she is chilling with ya girl, and she is talking about how she can't fuck with you nigga." He burst out laughing.

"Oh, we gonna see. I'm bout to pull up don't snitch, nigga." I jumped up and walked outside.

"Nigga, we are coming too. I'm about to spit my shit too. Trez said they gotta a friend with a whole lot of ass," Bleek said.

"We'll have Ava come get yo shit nigga if you riding," I said.

"Man, hell nah. I'll just follow yo ass. Ava's been tripping lately."

"Yeah, since you fucked the bitch and kept it pushing, she's been bugging since then, nigga." Trez pushed Bleek laughing.

I ain't see shit funny cause I made it clear she was off limits. Ava was my bad ass assistant that wanted to fuck her way to the top. She was amazing at her job, and I really haven't had time to find anyone else, so I needed Bleek to dead that shit, or I would have to let her ass go.

"Man, what the fuck did I say? You keep on fucking any and everything and you gonna get fucked up. Now I gotta let her ass go." I wiped my face and started my Benz. "If y'all coming, let's go."

"You really doing this, man?" Trez asked.

"Shit, Octavia wanna play, so I'm about to show her who daddy is and what happens when you play with a real nigga." I smirked.

Once they were in the car, we were on the way to Bella's crib. Trez had already let us know her parents were gone, and they were trying to hit the mall but hadn't left just yet. Pulling up to where I dropped Octavia off earlier, I texted her phone telling her to come outside. Trez must have hit Santana too cause all three came out. Santana and Bella were giggling while Octavia had this smug look that I didn't like.

Walking up to her, I tried to wrap my arms around her waist, but she moved back on a nigga, I was confused cause just earlier we were good. "Wassup, why you acting all mean now?" I asked.

"Look, I know we had a good time Amir but..." She stopped and saw everyone looking at us.

"Yeah so choose ya words wisely lil lady cause I ain't wanna be embarrassed, and I been bragging." I smiled.

"Can we talk in the car?"

Walking over, I opened her door and then got in. "Wassup, lil lady?"

"Look, Amir, I like you I really do, but I don't think right now I need to be with anyone. You're smart, good-looking, and sweet, but I just stop my drama with Omari, and I don't wanna bring you any since y'all work together. I ain't that female, plus I'm going to school soon, and I don't wanna have anything holding me back," she stated, looking me in my eyes then quickly looking down at her phone.

"I can understand that, but one me and Omari don't work together. He wanted me to put him on, but he's too sloppy, and I didn't like how he handled you, so he's done. For two, I enjoyed my time with you too Octavia, and I honestly can't let a good thing like you go. As far as school, you got my support. Go get your degree, and I'll be right by your side as long as you're for sure by mine. I ain't with the games lil lady, so when I said you were mine, I meant it," I said and pulled her onto my lap. I kissed her tasting the wintergreen gum she had in her mouth.

My baby was perfect, and by the way she was grinding on my mans, I knew she was just scared of how her past treated her. I planned to show her that us niggas ain't built the same, and I was gonna send her to the top with me.

"So, what are you doing here anyway?" she asked, playing with my hair.

"I heard you were trying to diss my ass, so I had to show and prove for my niggas. What you about to get into, I thought we had plans?"

"We do? Oh, I forgot. Let me ask my girls, hold on." She rolled the window down and told Bella to come here.

"If this nigga gets his thirsty ass out my face maybe I could get there. Move Bleek I am good on your hoe ass," Bella cursed, walking to the car. "Uh-uh, why you all on him like that?" She frowned, making us both laugh.

"Amir wants to chill, what are you thinking?"

"Well, shit, y'all look like y'all made y'all choice," she said, nodding towards Trez and Santana who were kissing on the hood of his truck.

"Girl, you better entertain Bleek. He looks like he is really feeling you."

"Girl, he would feel a fish if it had a pussy. I ain't fucking with his hoe ass. I'll go, but Amir you better have some good smoke and something strong to drink," she said and hopped in the back.

After telling Trez and Bleek the plans, we rolled out. The girls wanted food, so we picked up Chinese and pizza and hit the highway. Bleek rode with us, so he and Bella were in the back seat talking shit back and forth. Me and Octavia just kept laughing. If they didn't see it, we did, and we knew they were meant for each other.

Pulling up to my estate and getting inside, me and my niggas watched the girls tour the house. My phone buzzed, and it was a text from one of my lil niggas. Getting the men, we went to my office while the girls finished their tour. Watching Octavia show my house made me feel like she was meant to be here. It also made me think she needs her own space too.

Getting into my office, I got straight to business. "I guess that nigga really wanna test me."

"What you mean, bruh?" Bleek stepped up.

"That bitch nigga Omari hit two of my spots after the meeting. His niggas dropped Kasey, and Erica and Pook are in the hospital as we speak," I fumed. This nigga really wanted me to end his shit and send him to his bitch ass pops.

"You think his family is helping him out?" Trez asked calmly. Trez was the silent killer. He didn't speak; he just acted out.

"Nah I doubt they even know baby boy is on the loose right now," I stated.

"So, what's the move, my nigga? You know I stay ready," Bleek said.

"Yeah, we gonna chill. Let that nigga think he's good but make sure they find his ass. We're gonna chill with our ladies, and then we get his ass," I said. If that nigga thinks he got away, then he had another thing coming. He got my ass for fifty G's and ten keys, so he knows he a dead man.

"Shit, he's probably at the bus station right now B," Trez said just as a light knock at the door came.

"Come in babe; it's open."

"I just wanted to know if y'all were ready to eat. Tana's making plates, and Bella's making shots and rolled for us," she said so sweetly smiling at me.

"Yeah, we coming right now," I said, and she left out. "Yeah, we'll handle his ass after I get my baby straight. For now, have our lil niggas out here looking for him. Try that bitch Janet's house. I know she's gotta know," I said, and we went to find the girls.

Chapter Eight

OCTAVIA

After hearing Amir and the guys talk about going after Omari, I had to get my plans in motion. I heard him say he was gonna be on the run which gives me some time for my plan of action. Mari thought he was getting away with raping me and leaving me for dead, but I was coming for his ass. I just had to get to him before Amir did.

We had chilled with the guys, and Trez was about to take us home, but Amir wasn't trying to let me leave again. "Babe, I have work in the morning and if I ain't home my momma's gonna trip, trust me," I said, kissing him on his forehead.

"Man, iight I'll take you home then. You had a nigga thinking he was gonna get some time in with his girl in this big ass house by myself, huh?"

"Well, you could always downsize, Amir. You had this before me, so it's not on me." I stuck my tongue out getting up from his lap. He grabbed his keys, and we met them at the cars. Amir and I drove to my house while Trez and Bleek took my girls home. As I pulled up, I could feel Amir staring at me.

"What?" I asked, looking back at him.

"Man, there you go. I can't just look at my girl?"

"Yeah, but you're staring that's different," I stated. I hated to be stared at cause I still had some insecurities.

"I'm just enjoying the beauty within baby that's all," he said and gave me and peck on the lips.

"Well, I'm going in. Text me and let me know you made it home safe."

"Will do," he said and pulled off.

I walked inside, and my parents were both gone. It was about ten, so I knew my mom would be home soon and my dad after her. I texted Tana and Bella letting them know I was home and put my phone on the charger. I turned my Bluetooth speaker on and jumped in the shower. Letting the water run all over my body felt wonderful, and thoughts of Amir came into view. I could feel his hands all over me as the water massaged my body.

After washing up, I got dressed and got into my bed. I had to work in the morning, and I knew I couldn't afford to be late. Thankfully, Bella and Tana worked with me tomorrow so that I would have a ride to work. Our manager was really being a bitch, and I was ready to quit on her ass, but I needed the money for our townhouse in Charlotte. The girls and I figured why not move in together since we all got accepted to schools in Charlotte and that would keep us close should one or the other need anything.

I was just about to doze off when my phone went off letting me know I had a message. Looking, I saw it was Amir. Sitting up, he had let me know he had made it home and good night. Smiling, I locked my phone and went to bed. Time to deal with rude customers and management in the morning.

🦋

Waking up to a blaring alarm, I jumped into my closet to find my work pants. After failing, I just grabbed some black, straight legs pants and my slip-proof shoes and pulled my work shirt from off my desk chair. Brushing my teeth and then brushing my thick natural hair into a high bun, I buttoned up my work shirt and was out the door.

"Damn, why you always gotta have me late? Now Bella is on my ass about where we at," Tana fussed as I sat in the car.

"I'm sorry, best friend. I went to bed right after I got home. I was just tired I guess. Shit, I got some good ass sleep though." I laughed. "What did you and Trez end up doing?"

"Girl, nothing. He wanted some ass, but he already knows that's out till I am ready," she spoke driving to work. "But girl, if I ain't wanna jump on that big dick and ride it to glory! I felt that monster when we were in his truck."

"Damn, well you all in so you will. Girl, I don't know when I will even get that far with Amir. Going off subject though, Omari hit his spots for some money and work. I gotta get him before his lil niggas, Tana."

"I don't know how you plan to do that and you don't know shit about the game or finding niggas."

"Bitch, but I know family, friends, and hideouts!" I stated, "Even Amir don't know that, or does he?" I thought about it. The nigga knew about me before I even knew he existed.

"Well, like I said, I'm down. We just gotta plan this shit out. Where do you think he's at though?" she asked, pulling into the job parking lot.

"I think maybe Janet's sister house or his parent's business apartment out in High Point. That's where his family runs shit so that is where he would feel safe."

"Cool, well we will plan once we leave here, okay. I'll have Bella meet us at my dad's. Tamia and Maddison will be gone till about eight, and we get off at five, so we can at least have three free hours with no interruptions."

Thinking, we agreed and walked into work. Like clockwork, Tasha was on our asses as soon as we walked in. "Why are y'all thirty minutes late AGAIN?" she blared.

"Damn Tash, leave them alone. They're here now, so let's work," Bella said, wiping the front counter down.

"This is my shift, Kimbella. If you don't like how I run it how about you get off my clock?"

"That's no problem, but your dumb ass will be short so think twice cause you know ain't nobody else coming in when you call." With that Bella continued to wipe the counters, and Tasha rolled her eyes and us and went back to inventory.

❧

It was about 4:22 and I was wiping down tables for Bella since she decided to do drive-thru for me. We were supposed to get off at five o'clock, but Tasha was making me and Tana stay thirty minutes later for being late, talking about fucking up her labor. I hadn't heard from Amir since this morning when he sent me a good morning text, which I forgot to reply to because I was late for work. I made sure I set a reminder to call him on the way to Santana's dad's house.

Just as I put my phone up, I hear Soraya and Kaz's loud ass laughs come through the door. Soraya saw me and rolled her eyes, whispering to Kaz, and then they both laughed. Taking the high road, I went to put the bucket up and went to take their order.

"It's Bo Time, what can I get for y'all?"

"Ummm let me get a Cajun filet biscuit with fresh fries and a pie," Kaz said.

"Okay and for you?"

"Oh no, I'm good. My man won't let me eat this shit. He cares for my figure," Soraya said, twirling. "Speaking of, this is him calling now." She answered, and I went to fix Kaz order.

Just when I was giving Kaz her food, I could have sworn I head Raya say Amir on the phone.

"Can I have some honey mustard, damn?" Kaz yelled.

"If you asked nicely, damn," I said and tossed her the sauce. I was in no mood for their bullshit.

"Aww, what's wrong? You mad Amir dropped your fat ass for a real bitch?" Raya walked up smiling like she hit the jackpot.

"Nah, if that nigga wants you then you got him. I don't share; Janet saw that. Now would you like to order or are you gonna apply, but you can't occupy this area I have customers," I said and walked back to the cash register.

"Oh no daddy, Amir is taking me to lunch then I might just be his dinner." She giggled and walked out with Kaz laughing in tow.

I was pissed, and Amir had me fucked up if he thought he was about to play me like Omari, and I was giving my all. I know he wasn't getting pussy, but he claimed to be different, so this was showing me he lied. I finished my shift and let it go till I got off when I could really tell the girls. I didn't wanna be blanking and lose my job behind no nigga.

ﾷ

After clocking out, we drove to the park and ate our food. I wasn't even hungry after the day I had. I just needed to vent. "Amir is fucking Soraya," I said flatly, throwing my chicken back in the box.

"Wait, my sister Raya?" Tana asked.

I just nodded.

"How you know for sure?" Bella asked, lighting her blunt.

"She came in just for that. She and Kaz came to start some shit. That's probably how Mari found out he took me home that day."

"Nah, I don't think so, and if they did, it's in the past. I doubt he will fuck with her like that now that y'all are official," Tana added.

"Then why did my so-called man call her while she was standing in front of me?" I asked.

"Damn really? I can't believe this nigga. He's just getting in good and wanna fuck up already," Bella said, passing me the blunt.

"Right. He can have her ass, man. I ain't with that shit. Just cause you ain't getting pussy here, you gonna go after that. Nah, I am good."

"You don't know anything yet though, Tay. Have you spoken to him yet to get the man's side?" Tana asked suddenly being the peacemaker.

"No Tana I didn't ask him cause he's just gonna lie."

As if he could feel me talking about him, he called me. Sending him to voicemail, he called right back. We chilled and talked for a few then went to Tana house. Amir called again while we were getting into the house, so I answered and stepped back outside.

"What's up?" I dryly answered.

"Damn, it's like that now?"

"Yeah, it's like that now, especially when you have hoes like Soraya popping up at my job saying y'all fucking and going to lunch and shit. I don't share Amir so you can have that," I said, getting even more pissed.

"You done?"

"Am I done *ha-ha* yeah nigga I'm done! Enjoy ya day, iight," I said, hanging up and walking into the house. I wasn't about to let him play me like I was any regular bitch out here. I went up to Tana room and found them rolling up again.

"Damn, who pissed you off already?" Bella asked, lighting the blunt. She swears she doesn't smoke and she stays rolling lately.

"Amir's ass. Why call me if you ain't gonna say anything."

"What you mean? What did he say about him and Raya?" Tana asked, looking up from her phone.

"Oh, you're finally with us?" I joked. "He didn't say anything to defend himself honestly. I told him I knew and how shit played out and all he had for me was 'am I done'. I don't have time for the games. Mari played me long enough, and I won't accept it again from anybody."

"So he never got to explain the situation or give his side is what you're saying?" Tana said.

I knew where she was going and I didn't even want to entertain the bullshit. If Amir had nothing to hide and if he was the man he prides himself on being, he would come straight out and tell me.

"Santana, no he didn't get much out because I wasn't with the lies and the go around. As I said, he had time to say it was a lie or it was before me, or he was done with her ass, but no, instead he asked was I done like he didn't have to explain shit."

"So you won't feel dumb when that you find out he ain't fucking with her ass like that if that's the case, right?"

"Tay, all she's saying is you need to calm down and think. This shit with Mari and Janet has got you thinking everyone is the same, and that isn't always the case," Bella added.

"Well, I won't be around to find out. I hung up, and he hasn't even called or texted, so I guess he done too," I said, and with that, we kept on with our plan. We all figured we would use our time wisely and get the word from the streets since nobody we knew could find Mari.

We were tired as all get out when Maddison and Tamia finally got back home. Maddison said they were at Tamia's sister's house and she got to stay up late like us, while Tamia tried to get her upstairs and into the bath for bed. I loved little Maddison's spirit. She was always happy and didn't have a bad thought in her head. Hell, she even liked Mae's mean ass and gave her the utmost respect even when Mae show out.

Helping get Maddison to bed, we all ate, and the girls went to bed. I went and sat on the front porch scrolling through my Facebook when I saw Raya post a picture sitting in Amir's car. I took a screenshot and sent it to Amir hoping to get a reply out of him, but there was nothing.

Just as I was getting up from my seat, he texted me back, and I knew he had better have a good explanation. Opening my phone, all he had sent was the straight face emoji. Seeing that things weren't going anywhere, I went upstairs with the girls. Tana was still in her phone probably talking to Trez and Bella was eating hot Cheetos watching *The 100* on Netflix.

"Damn, what season are you on, Bella?" I asked, scooting next to her on the edge of the bed.

"Girl season two and you know they blew up Mount Weather, right? Killing all them people and Clarke done left them. They're all looking for her ass, while your ass in them trees with the grounders." She laughed, and I fell out with her. There was a character Octavia on the show, and she reminded me of myself except I knew when to run and when to fight.

"Oh, I must be past you then cause I saw all that, but I'll watch again. I don't have shit else to do. Tana, get out your phone, damn."

"I am dang. I don't even like this show and y'all know that."

She sat down, and we enjoyed the show back to back. Amir never texted or called me back, so I fell asleep trying to forget I even took that leap.

Chapter Nine

KIMBELLA WILLIAMS

W alking through the mall, I headed straight for GameStop to get Maddison a few new games for her Wii. Maddison's birthday is coming up, and Santana was trying to throw her a huge party. I swear Maddie was like her daughter more than a little sister, and I loved their bond.

Stepping inside and getting the games she had been talking about most, I went to the register. The guy ringing my things up was sweet and told me about a few games coming out that Maddie would like. I gave a stretched smile and continued to dig through my purse for my wallet.

"I got that, bae," I heard a deep voice behind me. Looking up, I rolled my eyes.

"Bleek, I don't need you paying. I have my own money," I hissed still digging for my wallet that I knew I put in my bag this morning.

"Damn, why you gotta be so damn mean all the time?" he said, passing the cashier the money while I grabbed the bags and began to walk off. "A thank you would work," he called out behind me.

Sitting in the food court, I finally found my wallet and took out what he had just paid. I walked around this damn mall for an hour and still didn't see Bleek's thirsty ass, so I decided to go ahead home. I could pay his ass back later. Walking to my car, I dropped my keys and went to pick them up. Out of nowhere, I felt a huge blow to my head making me drop the bags and fall scrapping my knee. When I turned around Soraya and Kaz was jumping my ass, so I kept swinging popping them both a few times. Out of nowhere Santana came out and pulled Soraya off me and started beating her ass like she stole something I mean Tana was giving her sister the work. I had taken my advantage and pounced on Kaziah's ass.

Just when I was giving her what she came for, I was lifted, but I sent a quick kick to her nose. "Yeah bitches, y'all came to play, and so did Bella!" I screamed, trying to get back at them bitches.

"Nah, you chill, ma. You're going home. Them damn security officers are on the way over. Get in your car and go. I got your bags," Bleek said in a deep ass tone that I didn't even wanna play with, but he would hear my mouth later.

"Yeah and bitch wait on me. I'll meet you at your momma crib, hoe!" I yelled and hopped in my Malibu and was out. I called Octavia to see where she was cause I needed a blunt and to figure out what's up now.

Pulling up, I saw a black Bentley pull up right behind me. Rolling my eyes, I got out and went to see what this nigga wanted.

"Bleek, I am fine. You don't have to keep tabs on me. I ain't your girl nor your little sister so go ahead," I said and walked away. I didn't have time for no nigga's shit, especially Bleek's ass. Even though he was fine as fuck and probably had a monster in his pants, I was good on that whole nigga.

"So that how you treat niggas who buy you gifts and save you from an ass whopping." He chuckled, but I ain't see shit funny.

Stopping dead in my tracks, I went inside my wallet and pulled out the money I put to the side and handed it to him.

"Here, don't just look at it. You're so pressed for a hundred dollars here! This is exactly why, man," I huffed, but he just stared at me with this smirk. As mad as I was I couldn't take it out on Bleek cause he was right. This man had helped me out twice today and here I was being an ass.

"Look, I know you are having a rough day, and I just wanna make it better, beautiful. Obviously, you've been hurt, or someone broke your trust, but I ain't that nigga, and I swear I'm going to show you that." He pulled me in and kissed me softly then went and got in his car, leaving me there wet and confused.

"But that thirsty nigga won't get me though," Tay mocked me, laughing.

"Bitch, first off, fuck you. And two, he still doesn't have me! That kiss was nice though, so we gonna play. Bleek is a hoe, and you know this, so I don't plan on giving my all until he gives his." We both burst out laughing. "And we know that won't happen."

"I don't know, Bella. You would be surprised how a man can change when they really want something or someone."

"Ain't that the pot calling this kettle black?" I asked, rolling my eyes. Here Tay was telling me Bleek could be a changed man for me but won't believe the same for her and Amir.

"Ugh with Amir it's different, and you know why. I just got done with Omari and Janet, and I have to watch her get bigger day by day." She started to tear up, so I pulled her in for a hug. "Don't get me wrong B, I really am feeling Amir, but it's been two whole weeks, and I haven't spoken to him. Maybe it was just a phase?"

"Octavia, you haven't spoken to him because you haven't picked up that phone to reach out. You're so stuck on being right and making this nigga out to be a dog that you can't see he might be able to change too. Shit bitch, y'all only dated for three days and you cut him off over some hearsay shit."

"Hearsay from the biggest hoe in North Carolina, right B? Okay, I might be wrong, but I don't know how to go about apologizing to him. Hell, all them rides to and from his house, and I still don't know how to get out there."

"Well, how about I fix that. Come on let's go in. I gotta fill you in anyway."

We went inside, and I told Tay all about the fight and how it started. As I already knew Santana had already called and filled her in but was staying with Trez for a little while. We chilled and smoked until about five, and then I decided to head home.

I swear this was the thing I dreaded most going to this place called home. My life growing up was nothing. That's the only way to sum up my childhood. I mean it wasn't all bad, at least when my grandmother was alive. See my dad had a drinking problem that only she could tame, and it wasn't bad, it was scary.

My dad wasn't the hit on me or talk shit type of drunk; he was the funny drunk that falls and hurts himself drunk. When my family or I try and talk to him, he just tells us we not lit like him and keeps with his drinking. Just two months ago, I had to leave work because my neighbor found him on the porch with a gash on his forehead. I was afraid to lose my dad; he was all I had. I never knew my mother, and for all I know she was somewhere with some man who didn't want kids in his big ass house.

Stepping into my house, I could feel the devil throwing five more weights on each shoulder. The house was a mess; I could see pizza boxes from the couch to the kitchen doorway. They had beer bottles and cans that had fallen out of the trashcan leaving the rest exposed with flies flying everywhere. To top it off there was still food, drinks, and clothes covering the floor.

"Dad, when I finish cleaning this mess your behind is mine!" I yelled down the hall as I began picking up stuff and throwing it in a huge garbage bag. When I didn't hear anything, I ran back to his room and found him on the floor on his back. Hurrying to my phone, I called 911 and gave them the address and ran back to my dad.

"Dad, just stay with me, they're coming. You hear me? They're coming, daddy. Just stay don't leave... please don't leave me!" I cried as the sirens got closer.

When the medics came in, I showed them the room and watched as they put an oxygen mask on him and yelled for a roller bed. I called Tay and Tana so they could meet me at the hospital. We were almost inside when I heard one of the paramedic's yell, "Let's go! I'm losing him!"

When we arrived at the hospital, they rushed him to the back, and I was right with them. They weren't going anywhere without me, and I dared anybody to touch me or think about the shit. This was my damn daddy, and I was going to be right there. We came to double doors, and the OR doctor came out and told me I must go to the waiting area.

"Hell no. Like I told the men back there, he's not leaving me! MOVE so I can go with my daddy!" I shouted with tears falling as I watched them pushing him into surgery. Looking back at the doctor, I pushed him as hard as I could. "MOVE, JUST MOOOVEE!" I screamed. I was being held back, and I finally gave up and turned around and let it all out.

I didn't know the status of my dad or what was even wrong for him to need surgery, but I knew I was losing a war I didn't know I was fighting. I looked up, and Bleek was staring right back at me. He didn't say anything, he just picked me up and carried me to the waiting area with Santana and Octavia.

We had only been in the waiting area for maybe an hour and ten minutes, but Bleek never left. He would go ask for blankets and got us some snacks, but he sat right with us never saying a word. I was grateful they were here with me, and once I made sure my dad was okay, I was going to give Bleek that shot. Hopefully, he could wait on me. If not, it is what it is. I have my daddy.

Finally, the same doctor came out asking for the Washington family. "Sorry about earlier Dr. Stephens, but that's my world back there, and I needed him to be okay, and I didn't want to leave him," I started off.

"You're fine. I understand. It happens a lot, and we can't control our emotions when it comes to those we care most about. Your father is fine. We only took him back to surgery because we noticed bruising on his stomach and noticed his hernia. Was this something that might have been giving him some trouble?" he asked.

"Thinking back he did say the other day he wasn't feeling good. He had been in bed since then, but he never said anything about a hernia."

"Well, we took care of it. We want to keep him just to observe him a day or two, and then he can go home. You all can go back when they bring him from recovery."

"Thank you again, Dr. Stephens." He shook my hand and went on his way.

I thanked everyone for coming and told them they could leave. My family hauled ass, but Santana and Tay said they were waiting with me and went to get us some food. I saw Bleek sitting down, so I joined him.

"Thank you, Bleek. For real," I said.

"Nah, that's my job. I had to make sure you were alright. When Tana got the call, Trez let me know, so I came. Is ya ole man okay?"

"Yeah, he's good. It was a damn hernia that he was hiding from me. Can you believe that?" I chuckled.

"Aye, it made you smile though, so think about it like that."

"Yeah, but the same way he instilled in me that I can come to him for or about anything I expect the same respect," I said, tearing up again.

"He's good Bella, now go back there and chop it up with ya pops. I have some moves to make, but I'll bring y'all some food, iight?" He kissed my forehead, and I nodded. Tay and Tana passed him walking out with trays in their hands.

"I know that ain't no café food, bitch?" I turned my nose up.

"Is you hungry or is you ain't?" Tay mocked.

"She looks like she high off Bleek to me Tay," Tana joked.

"Girl, he got me over here good. He calms me." I rolled my eyes. "Tay that plan better still be in motion for tomorrow. Daddy is fine, so we gotta make that move."

"I don't know y'all what if it doesn't work? What if Amir is done with me? I mean I was really childish, and it's been two damn weeks. I don't wanna seem thirsty," she said slouched down in the chair.

"No, you're making things right. If you want him, take him. Don't ask for permission. Give that nigga a taste of his own medicine, and he will be yours. If not, the next bitch will have him and more."

"She's right Tay. I hate to say it, but if Soraya will snatch and attack for him, then that means she wants him bad. Amir is cool and laid back. He's got his head on straight, and he's really feeling you. Go ahead and do you boo. Getcha man, girl," Tana said, and Tay looked relieved.

After talking a bit more, the nurse came and got me to go sit with my daddy. When I got back there, he was knocked out cold, so I pulled his covers over him and turned the lights down. I kissed him on the forehead and pulled out the couch bed and laid down. Since I wasn't sleepy, I put Bleek number to use and texted him the tongue out emoji. I wanted to play.

Chapter Ten

AMIR

It had been two weeks since Octavia blanked on a nigga over the phone. I had to look at my shit to make sure it was her ass cause we had just hit it off a few days before. I knew fucking with Soraya ass was going to catch up with me, but anything that happened between us was before Octavia.

Yet, here I was again getting the skin sucked off my dick, and Raya was doing her thing when my phone went off.

"FUCK!" I said just as I released down her throat.

All Soraya ass will ever get is my dick down her throat for the shit she pulled. When she ran her mouth, I hadn't been fucking with her for weeks at that point, and she knew it would fuck up me and O.

I checked my phone and saw that it was O telling me to meet her at this address, and we needed to talk. "Aye, you gonna have to gone head. I gotta make a run," I said, texting O back.

"Damn, it's like that? When are you gonna let me ride that monster again, daddy?" Raya purred.

"If you don't get out my car I'ma call my lil niggas to run that shit dry. Now get the fuck out Raya, I got moves to make."

"Man, fuck you, Amir!" She got out slamming my car door. I sped off. Don't nobody care about Raya's spoiled ass. I might be getting my girl back, so fuck her.

🙚

Pulling up to the hotel, I called Octavia and got the room number. She was staying in the Marriot downtown, and I was trying to see how she got the money cause Tana told us how she hadn't been going to work since we started talking.

I knocked on the door, and she opened the door for me to walk in. Observing the room, I knew she had to spend some bands for this shit. Turning around, I went to confront her, and lil lady had on a black lace set with some black heels on. I swear my dick rocked up so hard. She had her hair blown out and curled. She didn't have a face full of makeup as usual, and I loved that shit.

"Amir, I know I went off on you the other day," she started, walking up to me and rubbing my mans like she was ready, "And I know you just wanna make me feel better, right?" she purred into my ear.

"That was my plan, but not like this, O. I ain't fucking with Raya, and I haven't been since we started talking. I want you and only you and I meant that shit."

"What you mean not like this?" she seductively said, releasing my dick from my sweats

"Shit O, chill bae, not till you ready."

She dropped down and took me all the way down her throat, something ain't no bitch ever been able to do with my shit, not even Raya's hoe ass. She sucked and slurped on my dick, and when she started moaning on my shit, I had to hold her head back a little to keep from busting.

"You said you wanted to make me feel better right, Amir?" The way she let the 'R' roll off her tongue had a nigga ready to add a ring to this make-up session.

She got on the bed and now it was my turn, I buried my face in her pussy and went to work. My baby taste so fucking good and sweet that I couldn't stop. He legs shook, and she tried to get away, but I had a firm grip, and I needed more. After she came all over me, I climbed on top of her.

"You sure you ready, O?" I asked seriously.

"Yes, make love to me, Amir."

With that, I stroked my mans slow and deep while she dug her nails into my back. The sounds of her moans were like Jazz music. She had me feeling a whole different way.

After a while, O started to match my thrust, I pulled my dick out and turned her over. I began to eat her pussy from the back, and just before she was about to cum, I eased back into her and sped up my pace.

"Fuck yessssss! Juuussttt like that, Amir! Make me feel that shit, baaaabbyyyy!" O screamed, and I could feel her squeezing my dick.

"You tried to leave me, O?"

"Yessss, but I didn't mean... oh shiiiittt, Amiirr!"

"Nah, talk that shit, O!"

I fucked her long and hard until my baby passed out on me. I never thought this was how we would fix things, and it wasn't my plan. I still needed Octavia to know that I wanted to be with her. Gently, I shook her to wake her up.

"Round two later, babe. You wore me out," she whined.

"Look, I just want you to know that this means a lot to me that you did this, but I need to know that you want to still be here. I'm really feeling you O, and I wanna be the man you need, but I also want to be wanted. I ain't fucking with Raya. I used to, but that was before I met you. I'm serious about us if you are."

"What are you saying Amir, cause these past few weeks have been hell. You became my best friend in a day, and then that drama started. You know sitting in that hospital watching Bleek be there for Bella made me think about all the times you were there for me. Amir, I love you not for what you seem to have, but for always being there," she countered never losing eye contact.

"Damn, so you in love with the kid, huh?"

"No, I said I said I have love for the kid, he's gotta earn the rest."

She kissed my lips making my mans rock up again, and like clock-work, she went down and gave me what I needed. That was the thing about O. She had a nigga open, and I needed to keep that on the low. Niggas see her and know that's me, so the last thing I needed was to have something happen to her behind my doings.

I sat there and watched her sleep, and I thought about Omari. The nigga had been missing for a whole month, and there was still no new info on where this nigga could be sleeping. I needed to handle his ass before anything else popped up. Pulling out my phone and stepping outside, I called Trez and Bleek and told them to meet me at the diner across the street.

"So our niggas still ain't found this kid, huh?" Bleek asked.

"Nah, I got lil Moochie on his ass, and he said his lil homies are down to play, so they're holding shit down. Now, where he hit us we got back, so we're not tripping, but I need this nigga dealt with so that I can know I've been paid back!"

"Shit you know he took Janet with his ass, right? Her own momma doesn't know where she's at right now," Trez added, eating some eggs. "But, I saw lil mama at the doctor's office when I went and picked that thing up," he finished.

"So did you speak to her, nigga?" Bleek asked.

"Nah, I ain't want her getting suspicious since she knows we are looking for his ass."

"True so what are you thinking, Amir?"

"Look, we gonna let him come to us. I know that nigga is running dry and can't have a connect yet, so once all that work is gone and my nigga needs a check, he's gone pop up trying to get more. That's when we hit his ass. Iight?" I stated. I don't need his punk ass running again.

We chopped it up in the diner for a bit, and then I headed back to the room. I was ready for round two and O better be up and ready. When I got to the room, she was having a nightmare, so I rush to wake her up.

"Bae, you good?" I asked holding her, but she didn't say a word. She was quiet and shaking.

"Yeah, just lay with me please?" she finally whispered.

I knew it was more to that nightmare because I heard her saying Omari's name. The shit fucked me up cause he had a hold on O, and that shit wasn't gonna work. My girl should never fear another nigga cause she should always feel safe.

"O, you know I got you, right? I don't know what that shit was about, but I got you and ain't nobody gonna ever hurt you as long as I got breath in my body," I said, pulling her face to mine so that she knew I was serious. "All you need to worry about is going to school next month and shutting them classes down. I got the rest. I just want you to be happy and live, iight?"

"Thank you, Amir. Look, that night did something to me. I will never forgive him for that, and I don't think I will ever be that girl again. That nigga didn't break me, and you are right, I will go to school, and I plan on finishing top of the class. I promise, I'm fine, babe," she stated and kissed me, slipping her tongue into my mouth making my mans rock up.

She climbed on top of me, and I sat up so that I could suck and lick all over her nipples. I loved my girl and how confident she was. I couldn't help but feel all over her as she grinded on my dick.

"Stop playing, Amir," she moaned, causing my dick to jump. I swear she fucked up. I was gonna make her feel better by any means.

I slid my dick inside her and guided her while she rode. I knew she wasn't a pro, but O was handling business. She was twirling her hips, and when her shit tightened around my dick, I had to sit up. "Shit O, ride daddy just like that, bae."

"Like this, daddy?" she moaned, speeding up.

She started bouncing on my dick and then threw her head back. I knew she was about to cum, but I wasn't done with her ass yet. I began to match her back, and she went crazy. I pinched her nipples, making her bite her lip.

"Yes daddy, just like that!" she screamed.

"Cum all over daddy's dick, O, gimmie what I want."

"I'm coming Amir, FUCKKKK!" She fell over me, and I couldn't hold back my chuckle.

Laying her down in front of me, I eased my dick in from behind her. She softly moaned as I stroked her deep and slow.

"Baeeeeee, I'm sleepy," she moaned.

"The way this pussy is squeezing me, I don't think she's done, bae."

"Amir, that's myyyyy... ohhh shiiiit!" she let out as she came all over my dick. I sped up my pace making her scream and shout. Feeling my nut rise, I pushed her down and continued to pound on her spot.

"Cum with daddy, O," I groaned in her ear, biting down on her neck and ear.

"Yeesss DADDDYYYYY right therrreee!!!" she moaned as she came all over me. I kept going till I finally released my seeds in her. I didn't care I wasn't wrapped cause I knew Octavia would hold me down.

We got up and went to shower, which turned into another session. I couldn't get enough of O, and I knew my bae was addicted to me. I knew I was done at this point. This is what I wanted to come home to, wake up to, and go to bed next to. O was gonna be my forever, and she didn't even know it. It was time that I made some moves to secure our future.

"O, what you think about a lil vacay before you go off to school?" I asked as we laid on the new sheets. I knew she wasn't asleep cause she was quiet.

"That would be nice. Where are you trying to go?"

"I'll just plan the trip, and you just be ready and packed by eight a.m. next Friday, iight. I got this," I said, reaching for my wallet on the nightstand and handing her my card. "This is for you to get some new gear. There's no limit. Everything is on me, bae. Just get what you want."

"Amir, I think I have some things already. I don't need anything else." She giggled.

"Well, that's still all you, so take the girls and all y'all go find some shit and have fun. That's all I was saying, bae."

"Iight, I'll call Tana and Bella tomorrow and see what they have planned then. Thank you, baby." She kissed me and laid back down.

I had more in store for her, and I couldn't wait to see my baby face when she see it all. Kissing her forehead, I fell asleep holding my forever.

Chapter Eleven

OCTAVIA

The past few months had been the best of my life. Amir took me on the trip of a lifetime. We visited Costa Rica, and everything about it was amazing, including the blue skies, clear blue waters, and the food. Yes, a bitch enjoyed the food the most. Amir surprised me and had Trez, Santana, Bella, and Bleek join the trip, so I knew I would have a ball.

We drank, smoked, and ate the whole trip. I don't think I was ever sad or mad the entire trip. I can't speak for everyone cause Bleek and Bella were steady going back and forth one minute, and then good the next minute. Bleek swore she needed some act right, and I think he gave her just what she needed. I must say these niggas got my girls and me glowing up these streets.

This week I will be leaving the nest. And since I had been basically spending my summer with the girls and Amir, as well as going back and forth to Charlotte, I decided to chill with my parents for a while. To be honest, I had been avoiding the awkward presence that surrounded my house these past few weeks. My mom had been very depressed, and my dad was hardly home.

Walking into the kitchen, I saw my mom was cooking breakfast. I walked up behind her and hugged her. My mother was beautiful, and although she gained a few pounds throughout the years, her beauty never left. I saw myself in my mother. Back in the day, I heard everyone wanted my momma, but she had eyes only for my dad. They had been together since high school, and I hoped they continued, but Amir was right maybe they needed their space.

"Hey, Ma, what are you in here cooking?" I asked, leaning on the counter.

"The stranger is hungry, huh?" She chuckled. "I made grits, eggs, bacon, and biscuits, but they aren't done yet Octavia, so don't go messing with my food."

"Ma, I know not to touch your food while you're cooking, dang." I laughed then snatched a piece of bacon and slid into the dining room.

"I see you Octavia; you ain't slick!"

"Deduct it from my plate, Ma. I'm starving, and I need a home cooked meal."

"So cook. You know how, so don't act like that."

"I know Ma, but it's not the same as your cooking? How you been though?" I asked, taking a sip of some water.

"I've been baby, that's about all I can say. Dealing with the blessing the Lord has given that's all." She looked away and got up to check on her biscuits.

"Well, what about you and dad? I didn't forget Ma, and you can just leave me in the dark."

"We're fine, Octavia. We talked, and I decided I wanted a divorce."

"Just like that, Ma? You ready to throw in the towel?"

"Baby, I love your father with all of me and the last thing I see myself doing is throwing in any towel. Your father isn't happy with me anymore Octavia, and instead of begging and pleading, making myself feel less of a woman, I'm letting go. I want us to both be happy and you too. Now, I know it hurts, but we are still your parents and will love you all the same. He will still be living here until things are finalized, and he finds a place. I wouldn't do him dirty. Even if he has been doing me dirty, that's still my husband, and I still have duties as a wife."

As mad as I wanted to be, I had to respect what my mom just said. She wasn't giving up. She was giving him the space he asked for without a fight.

"I understand, where's dad?"

"In the room watching *SportsCenter* as always. You know he's been trying to convince me to purchase that *WWE* pay-per-view?" She chuckled lightly.

I walked up to her and hugged her again. I could smell her natural sweet scent that used to put me to bed at night. I didn't want to let go, but I knew she would be okay. I was truly afraid to leave my mom here alone.

I walked into my parent's room and just like my mom said he was sitting on the edge of the bed watching *SportsCenter*. "Hey, pretty girl. I heard your momma talking about my pay per view. Is she gonna get it?" he asked.

"No, daddy. She ain't biting so you might be stuck, and don't ask me, I will not get in between y'all TV drama."

"The only reason she won't get it is cause that damn *Scandal* comes on and she acts like she can't see it later."

"Daddy, she told me y'all getting a divorce. I'm sorry, daddy." I leaned in and hugged him so tight. I loved my father because right, wrong, or indifferent he was my father.

"Aww baby, don't dwell. I messed up, and I know she tired of my sorry's. She deserves some peace. She thinks I ain't happy, but that wasn't even the case. I just need to give her some time, baby. We gone be alright."

He kissed my forehead just as my mom walked in with his plate stacked with food.

"That's right we will be just fine once our daughter goes off to college." She beamed, sitting his plate down in front of him.

I sat back and watched as he ate and she sat back pulling out her Kindle and started to read a book. My parents have always been the run to parents. When my friends had issues, they ran here. I don't know what life will bring them both, but I hope it's pure happiness.

I sat with them for a little while longer and then went to pack a few things up. Amir had already told me we were going up a week early to get some stuff ready for classes, and I needed to make sure I was ready. I swear he hated when I was late, but loved when I made up for it, so I knew I was good.

Going through my things, I found the pictures of Omari and me from years ago and got upset once again. The nightmares haven't stopped, and each night it stays the same. I dream that I am with Tana and Bella and Mari comes out of nowhere and shoots them in the head. Right before he kills me, he tells me it's all cause of me. I had to find his ass before I left. I wasn't going to school with this nigga still running wild.

I ripped up the pictures and got my stuff together. I called the girls and told them it was time to move. I knew if anybody knew where he was it was Janet and she was due for an appointment soon. One thing he messed up at was knocking up a social media hoe. Every move they made she posted— doctors' appointments, baby shopping, and going out to eat like niggas wasn't looking for Mari's weak ass.

Just as I was finishing up, I gotta message from Bella saying they were outside. I told my parents I was gone and asked if they needed anything before I left. Making sure they were good; I was out. We pulled right up to the office and waited.

"I know this bitch better not play today cause pregnant and all she can still catch this shit," Bella said, turning up the A/C.

"I doubt it, man. She's so ready for the baby to get here the most she is gonna do is talk shit. She ain't with the shits, not with us," I said, dapping up Tana at the same time Trez walked right up to her window and bent down cheesing.

"Damn, you just make boss moves, huh?" I heard Amir say from behind me, and I froze. How did they even know we were here? "Don't get quiet on me now, O. Come on, let's go," he said calmly.

"No, Amir. I got something to handle. You should know that better than anyone, right?"

"O, I said let's go, and if I have to yank your ass out this car I will, but this weak ass stake out is dead. Now let's go!" he said in a tone I had never heard, at least not with me.

Getting out the car, I got in his and slammed the door. I took my phone out while I waited for him to come to the car. Here I was trying to handle my damn business, and he's in my face.

He got in the car and sped off, never taking his eyes off the road and never said anything to me. He got on the highway and headed towards Charlotte, and finally turned the radio on.

"Amir, you ain't gonna explain why or even how knew you to pulled up on us today?" I asked words filled with attitude. Nothing. "So you don't hear—" and he cut me off by turning the radio up.

We drove for about two hours when he finally pulled up to a secluded housing development. There was a huge gate that surrounded the houses, and security posted all around. We entered, and the houses were beautiful. We drove all the way to the back and down a driveway so long that I thought it was another street. When we finally reached the house, I looked at Amir and said, "Well, somebody might have outdone your house, babe."

It was huge; I mean amazing. My house at home wasn't bad, but it wasn't this! I walked around the front of the house just admiring its beauty. It was a ranch style mini-mansion in my opinion, with black on white décor all around. The grass was green, and the flowers were pink and yellow around the porch. There was a swing on the front porch, and it reminded me of my grandma's house.

"Come on. Let's go in." was all he said.

Rolling my eyes. I walked ahead and waited at the door for him to open it. When he did, I fell in love. As soon as you walk in, you see the staircase leading you either up or down. We walked straight through and was inside the kitchen. The kitchen was black and platinum everything. It had an island and a bar included. The dining area was big enough to invite families to Thanksgiving.

"This is you, O," Amir said, walking up and holding me from behind.

"What you mean this is me, Amir? I cannot afford this, and why would I even need all this space for just me and you?" I asked looking at him dumbfounded.

"This is us, bae. It's close to the school, and I got the payments. I just ask that we fill this bitch up with babies when you ready."

"Oh, my gosh, Amir. I love you so much, thank you!"

"You're welcome, but about earlier, why are you trying to mess with Janet, O?"

"Them nightmares are getting to me, Amir. Now I know you are going after Omari, but don't you think I deserve some justice too? I mean fuck them traps getting hit. That nigga took something special from me, and I should end that nigga point blank," I said, looking him dead in the eyes. I wasn't playing or keeping it from Amir any longer.

"So when were you gonna let ya man who does this shit know ya moves, huh?"

"Amir, you are right, okay. I should have told you just in case you had a better plan, but baby I can't rest till that nigga dead," I said, tearing up.

"What's with ya nightmares, bae?"

I told him everything that happened in my dreams not leaving one thing out. He looked at me and didn't say anything at first. Then he smoothly got up and paced the floor. I had no idea what he had in mind, but I hoped he didn't leave me out.

"Look, I meant what I said, O. Your focus needs to be on school, not this bum ass nigga, iight? From now on you worry about school and loving me. Let me handle him, but what I will do is protect you, I'll have Bubz with you now, and don't protest. Other than that O, this is us," he said with his arms wide open. "This is what we worry about together, iight. I hold you down, and you hold me down. I love you Octavia Williams, and I promise you that I will find that nigga, and you will get what you want."

After hearing him say that, I knew Amir was basically cutting me out. I didn't want to fight or fuss, so I stood up and kissed him. I would focus on school no matter what, but he was a fool if he thought he was leaving me behind on anything. I rubbed his dick through his joggers, and he instantly jumped to attention.

I turned around and bent over the couch that was on display in the living room. Pulling my dress up, he smacked me on my ass and then dug into me, stroking me hard and deep.

"You know I gotta punish this pussy, right?" he groaned

"Yes, daddy, punish this pussy," I moaned back.

The way Amir would dick me down, I swore I was always a bad girl. He sped up, and in no time, I was coming back to back all over him. He never missed a beat, and when my legs started to give out, he caught my ass.

"Bae, I can't take it anymore."

"Nah you wanna do what you wanna do when you want to do it. Amir ain't shit to you, huh?" he said, laying me down on the couch and holding my legs up. He dug right back in and attacked my spot again. "Fuck O, this pussy is wetter than a muthafucka!"

"Amiirrrrr, slow down baby," I said, placing my hand on his chiseled chest.

"Nah, this is what happens when you forget who the boss is."

He fucked me until I was literally dizzy, and then had the nerve to try and help me to the bathroom. I loved Amir, but I really felt that maybe I needed this, and if he wanted to help that was fine, but he wasn't going to leave me out of it. I just had to come upon a new plan.

Chapter Twelve

SANTANA

Here I sat in my new house staring down at my second positive pregnancy test that I've taken. I didn't know what to think or say about it at the time, but I knew I was happy. Trez and I had been fucking like rabbits since the trip to Costa Rica, and I knew he had always talked about kids. Right now, I didn't know how he would take it I mean. I am just getting into school, and I start classes tomorrow. I don't think it's a good time to be starting a family, but I hoped Trez would be down.

Walking downstairs, I found Trez watching a movie and eating a huge sandwich. I went to sit on his lap, and when I went to kiss him, I felt my stomach coming up. Jumping up, I ran to the guest bathroom and threw up.

"Damn, my lil soldier in there giving you hell, huh?"

I turned to see Trez standing in the doorway with the test that dropped when I ran. "Yeah, I had the perfect way to tell you, but I guess the baby doesn't like my plans of action already."

"Tana, what are you thinking? We are keeping it right cause I got you, bae. I promise I got y'all. Neither of y'all will want for anything, you hear me?" he said, picking me up and taking me back to the living room. "If we're going to do this then we gotta do it right. You know I don't have any family, but you do have your dad 'nem that care about you. Say it's time we got to know each other, Tana."

"Trez, I don't think that's a great idea. I mean my dad can be kinda mouthy, and I don't have time for your ass when you get mad."

"Bae, that's pops point blank. He's ya dad I ain't going in there to disrespect or dishonor, but you're carrying my seed and want you to one day be my wife. When that time comes, I want to be man enough to go to your pops and ask."

I stared at him for a minute wondering where my thug ass boyfriend went, and when did this nigga pop up. "Okay I guess, but when I'm ready, okay?"

"You got it, but I get to tell my boys, man! Amir's about to be hot, brah!" he said jumping up and running upstairs. I had to laugh cause I swear I was supposed to be the hype one.

I picked up my phone and called Bella and Tay and told them to get over here right away. Thankfully, the men got us houses in the same development so we could literally walk to each other's houses. This was a blessing for me because I knew I would need their help with this baby. I loved Trez, but I also knew he had to work so that we could live and my man didn't work a nine to five.

I didn't want to be the nagging wife that knew what her husband did for a living and tried to put a time clock on it. I wanted to be his partner and the boss of the home front. As long as he wasn't out here fucking bitches and being disrespectful, we good.

About twenty minutes later the doorbell rang and in walked Bella and Bleek, fussing as usual.

"Nigga, kill that shit ain't nobody even on that anymore. All I asked was for you to take the trash on the way out. How do I sound like somebody momma?" Bella snapped.

"Man, whatever. You're always fussing, bae. It's always something a nigga ain't do right. When are you gonna love on a nigga, huh?"

"I loved on you all night Bleek, don't act like that." She winked.

"Umm eww, did y'all forget y'all were in my house?" I asked as they walked in. Bella sat beside me, and Bleek walked into my kitchen, as always.

"No. Bleek is just mad I stopped doing something to get here, but he knows what it is." Bella smirked.

"Bella, you better chill before I make you finish upstairs, Tana y'all got room so don't even cock your head around like that. This is my nigga shit too."

"Nigga and? You still won't get no pussy in this muthafuckas; the fuck you thought?" Trez said, coming downstairs looking like a pure snack. He had his fresh cut and his beard had grown, but he had it trimmed so nice. He had on some gray joggers that showed his long print.

"Wipe your mouth, bitch," I heard Tay say out of nowhere.

"Shut up Tay, and when did y'all just waltz into my shit?" I asked cause I damn sure didn't hear a knock.

"If you were looking we came in right behind they ass. Damn, with yo mean ass. Trez, go up there and handle that." She laughed. I threw her my middle finger, laughing with her.

"Well since y'all here I guess we can tell y'all first," I started.

"I'M GONE BE A POPS, Y'ALL!" Trez yelled, and everyone jumped up clapping and screaming. I had to side eye his ass cause I was gonna let it rip, but I remembered I did agree to him telling the guys.

"Congrats, Tana. I am so happy for you, my love," Tay said already rubbing my stomach.

"Yeah, Tana. We're happy for you, sis. Hopefully, your sister will give me a few soon too." Amir walked up and hugged Tay from behind. I loved watching them love each other. Tay deserved this happiness, hell we all did.

"Nigga you tried, maybe one day but not too soon," she countered and gave him a peck on the lips.

"Well, I already know I got a nephew on the way, so I'm good," Bleek said, taking a swig of his beer.

"How you know it's a boy, Bleek? What if it's a girl?" Bella asked.

"Shit, she's gonna be spoiled rotten, but that's Trez problem. Look at Tana, if that baby comes out looking like her ass, we're all going to war," Bleek joked and Amir laughing with him.

"Hell nah, ain't shit funny, my nigga. If she's carrying my princess, then she's going to be protected, straight up," Trez said not cracking a smile. That's my baby.

We had all finally sat down when one by one the guys' cells went off. They all jumped up, except Amir, and I looked at Tay for answers, but my best friend was just as lost as me.

Trez pulled me aside and took me into the kitchen, and I couldn't help but feel like something was wrong. "Bae, we gotta take a trip to the boro really quick. Some shit popped off, and I gotta handle some things, okay?" he said, and I couldn't hide the fact that I was upset.

"Right now, Trez? I mean damn we just announced our pregnancy and you out the door?"

"I know that bae and the last thing I wanna do is piss you off or stress y'all out, okay? It won't take me long. Go out celebrate with your girls. Matter of fact, here." He went into his pockets and gave me a wad of cash. "Y'all go shop and get your hair and nails done. When I come home, I want you to show me what you bought, iight?"

I just rolled my eyes and went back to the living room. I didn't want to feel some type of way, but I did, and I couldn't shake it. I sat next to Bella and just laid my head in her lap, I had to get out of this funk. He wasn't leaving for good; it was just a few hours.

"It's all good, Tana. Bleek is going too, and I understand it's business. Let go out; it's their loss. They gotta work baby, cheer up."

"I know I just wanted to celebrate this with him you know. I don't want to be the fussy baby momma, but I also want my man to be here with his family, especially something as big as this, Bella." I had to remind myself daily of the type of work Trez did and how it would have him out late and sometimes when I wanted him home.

"Whatever Amir, I will be with the girls when you get back. You ain't getting in here till you talking right." We heard Octavia fussing at Amir and then the front door close.

"What was that all about, Tay?" Bella asked. Both of us looking for answers.

"That nigga really got baby fever y'all. I knew Amir wanted a family — I mean a big ass family y'all, but I haven't even started classes yet. He's gonna have to give me some time."

"Damn, you mean as fuck, Tay. Why you kill that man dreams?"

"I don't think she is. I mean I understand her. Here I am carrying a child, and I feel like right now isn't the time. Don't get me wrong I will be having this baby, but it's crazy how I just got in school," I said, I understood Tay one hundred percent. We just got into school and started classes on Monday.

"How is Pops doing?" Tay asked Bella.

"He's driving me crazy, girl. Bleek's got him in a nursing home down here, and girl he's tired of the shit. We told him he could come stay with us, but he wasn't having that. He claims a man should be able to fuck when he wants to. Girl, Bleek's dumb ass dapped him up and thanked him. I just wanted him close so that I knew he was okay. He also can't drink in there, so you know he's hot."

We all burst out laughing, Bella's dad was a handful, but he loved us all the same. He never mistreated us and to be honest; he is the reason we all handle men the way we do. He put us up on game a long time ago. We talked for a little while longer and decided to hop out the house and go out. Concord Mall was always lit, so we jumped in my new Benz and was out.

We shopped until my feet felt like I had been standing on hot cinder blocks. Tay was hungry, and Bella wanted some ice cream, so we hit the food court for a much-needed break. I enjoyed being out with my girls, but I hadn't heard from Trez. I knew he should have made it by now, so I was wondering why I hadn't received a text or phone call. Putting my phone back in my purse, I gave the girls my attention.

"So basically I have to pass both classes to get into my majoring classes, I swear I want to change majors cause Criminal Science just seems so much easier." Bella laughed.

"I mean you talk to Bleek about it? What he say?" Tay asked.

"He was surprisingly down with the whole idea of switching. I mean to me he seems more on that side cause it helps them, but for me, I just want to do what I love to do, you know." Bella looked away, and I knew just like Tay did what she meant.

"Then go to hair school like you been talked about, Bella. You know that man will support you in anything you do." I took a bite of my burger and started to feel sick.

"Yeah, it's not Bleek that I was worried about, it's Pops. You know he wants me to be somebody nurse, lawyer, or doctor out here, I just don't feel like I want to be that. I mean I slay when I do hair, and my clients love me. I've picked up six clients since being down here, and that's great for a newbie to the city you know," she trailed off.

"Then do it, Bella. Tell Bleek, and I know we can help you make it happen. It's mad hair schools down here, and I know soon as you pass we can set up a shop. Yessss bitch, I need you to do this," Tay pushed Bella.

We all knew her potential, and we wanted her to be happy. Bleek was one step, and moving way from small ass Greensboro was another, but she had to do this.

"You guys are right. I know I got the magic touch and Tamia always said I had a booth in her shop. Maybe it's time I took that step y'all."

"Yup, and you know she's been looking at buildings here. She said she wanted something three stories with an elevator, but you know that stuff can be built in and daddy will do that. I think by the time you finish school it will be up, so maybe she puts you there," I said.

Tamia always looks out for us, and I know she would help Bella anywhere she needed the help.

"Ahhh, I am so excited. Thanks, y'all. I swear you guys are the best friends ever." Bella got up and hugged us.

"More like sisters. You're spoiled and then some girl," Tay joked.

"Yeah, that too." She kissed us both on the cheek and sat back down.

I looked at Tay waiting for info about Omari's bitch ass. The nigga was still hiding from Amir and his men, and I knew it wouldn't be long before he tried another stash hit.

"What, Tana? Amir's been all up my ass lately, so I can't plan shit. I have been thinking though of setting his ass up," Tay said, looking me dead in the eyes.

"What you mean Tay, cause this doesn't sound good at all," I said. I knew if couldn't do shit, and if Trez even knew I was over here plotting, that would be my ass.

"Well, I was gonna hit up Janet and tell her I wanted to apologize face to face since I didn't know she was pregnant. Janet being her, she going to tell Omari and he's gonna come not her. That nigga is so dumb that he will jump on the opportunity to see me and scare me."

"And when Amir's ass find out then what?" Bella asked

She got up and threw her stuff away and turned back to us, "Deny, deny, deny bihhhh." She laughed.

I knew this shit wasn't a good idea and Bella must have seen it all over my face. "Why are you looking like that, Tana?" she asked.

"I know you want to get his ass back Tay, but why not let Amir handle it? I mean you're technically down one girl remember?" I said, looking down at my stomach.

"Don't worry y'all. I got this. I've been hitting the gun range daily, and I told Amir it was just in case somebody got stupid."

"He ain't fall for that, Tay. You gotta match his wits, baby. Amir plays this game and has been for years. He took your lie and ran with it to bring up when your ass is caught," Bella said, laughing at Tay.

"Fuck! Damn Bella, your ass is right. That nigga played my ass." Tay laughed back.

"You know what I'm down and y'all can't talk me out of it. We going to get this nigga," I said, and they both fell out laughing.

"Nah mama, you're staying put. We do this with your ass involved and Trez will shoot us both. Nah you won't get us." The girls high-fived each other and laughed.

"Well, fuck y'all then I'll make sure I tell Amir everything with y'all bougie asses!" I poked out my lip and walked away.

"Aww, Tana we just can't take the risk baby. You're carrying our niece or nephew in there. It would kill us if anything happened to you, okay?" Tay said, hugging me.

I knew it was for the best but shit I wanted to feel included too. We finished up our shopping and decided to just chill in the crib. I didn't want to be home alone, so we chose Tay's house since she wanted to change clothes as well.

We stepped in, and Tay had done her thing. When we first saw the house, it was some white furniture in the living room, and now it was decked in black and gold. She had a plush carpet that my feet were calling for. Taking off my sandals, I went and hopped on the couch, and Bella joined me.

"What y'all about to watch?" Tay said, coming down the stairs in some peek-a-boo shorts and a tank top.

"Well, I wanted to finish up season three of *The 100*, but you haven't even gotten where we at," I answered.

"Damn, where you at? I just saw them kill Lexa!"

"Oh, we're passed that. I won't tell you. I'll just continue where you left off," Bella said starting the movie and rolling a blunt. I swear I wanted to hit that shit and just when I was about to ask Tay, her phone started ringing and so did Bella's.

I got up to check mine and still nothing. Looking up at the two, they wore stale faces, I knew nothing bad could have happened that soon, and I knew Trez was about to call with the news as well.

"So, what's up why are you looking like that? What did they say?"

"Omari hit they ass again when they went to secure the other spot. It wasn't him, but they say it was Mook and Tony, and they were driving Janet's old beat up Honda. Trez was shot Tana, but he's good. They're on the way now. They got him bandaged, so he's going to be okay," Tay said, walking up to hug me.

Pushing her back, I asked, "So he's hurt and y'all niggas on the way here instead of finding that pussy as nigga?"

"They making sure he's good Santana, chill." Bella stepped in between Tay and me.

"Nah, that nigga got on off in my nigga and y'all just running back here like he's some big nigga or something. Why are they not going after them bitches?"

"Cause they can't; they got niggas on them, Tana. Calm down before you stress yourself or that baby. They're almost here so we gotta get to your house to make sure he's good," Tay said, getting her things together as well as Bella.

"Nah, I got my nigga from here. Y'all stay, would hate for anything to happen there." I said and gathered my things and left.

I didn't wanna hear them youngins were out looking cause they get popped easily. Amir had the reach to find his ass and put a stop to it but hasn't. They didn't want to hear it, but if Trez wasn't good, I was going to find the nigga my damn self.

Chapter Thirteen

SORAYA

*B**ANG, BANG, BANG!*
Jumping off the bed, I rushed to the front door and let Mook and Tony in my apartment. They dropped the bag and began to count.

"Damn, y'all hit two today?" I asked, getting excited. Two spots meant double the pay.

"Bitch, you made your cut clear. You're only getting the ten G's you asked for. If you got an issue, I can call Mari right now?" Tony barked.

"Aye, chill nigga. She told us where to hit, and we wouldn't have shit without her ass. Let finish counting," Mook said, winking at me. I smiled back and went back to my room.

I heard the front door open and slam shut, so I went to see what happened. If these niggas took my money and dipped, I was going to have Amir on they ass. Looking around, I saw on bag still on the table, but Mook and Tony had dipped. I went inside and counted five thousand and almost blanked.

Pulling out my cell, I called Janet's ass. "Bitch, y'all have me fucked up. You know this nigga will have my head if he knew it was me?"

"That has nothing to do with me, Raya. I didn't ask, Mari did, and you delivered. Damn, we have a child now, so we have to save our money too." She smacked her lips and hung up in my face.

I knew I should have just told Amir what I knew, but I wasn't even fucking with his ass like that anymore. In all honesty, he wasn't fucking with me. He had changed his number, and since he didn't do the whole social media ish, I knew he was gone. I had been seeing Tay and Tana posting him and Trez all over the book though.

I'd had enough of their shit, and this hit was the perfect payback, I wasn't done though. My sister always was the favorite with everyone except my momma, and I knew Trez was going to get hit. That's what he gets for choosing Tana's fat ass over me.

I had something for everybody, but I would have to sit on this five thousand and plan off that. Rubbing my protruding stomach, I swear I was ready for this shit to be over. I found out I was pregnant two months ago, and I didn't plan on telling a soul. The night Amir feel asleep in the room, I damn sure hopped on that massive dick and rode until I was geeked off it. If he had picked up, I would have told him about our little bundle of joy, but he couldn't even man the fuck up. Picking my phone back up, I called Santana. Mad or not I was still her sister, and I knew she would always break off for me.

"Hey Tana, don't hang up. It's Raya, and I need your help please." I played my best crying scene yet.

"Raya, what do you want? Your mess has been fucking up my life since I can remember and you have the nerve to call and ask me for something?" she huffed.

"I know Tana, and I just want to make things right. Ma kicked me out and I been staying with Kaz. I'm three months pregnant, Tana. I can't have this baby out here on the streets!" I begged.

"Ughhh, iight Raya, but at the first sign of some shit, you're gone. I'll text you the address, and you tell me when you're on the way."

"Tana?"

"What Raya, damn?"

"I'll need a ride too, please?"

"Be ready tomorrow. I'll be there around six after class." She hung up, and I jumped for joy.

The next day Tana pulled up as promised and we hit the highway, I didn't say a word, and she didn't either. I was trying to figure out my way around, but Charlotte was a big ass city. I really hadn't eaten anything all day, so I turned the radio down to actually talk to my sister.

"So, how you like it down here so far?"

"I mean it's okay. It's not the boro for sure, but it's home now. How far along are you, Raya?"

"Only a three months like I said. The baby is due February, so I won't be going into labor in your car, hell I ain't really showing like that."

She didn't reply after that, we just rode. We pulled up to an apartment complex, and I looked around cause this was not how I thought my sister was living. Shit was worse than what I had just come from.

"Tana, what's this shit?"

"Shut the fuck up Raya, damn. You ain't too good to be dropped off right here. The better ones are in the back. They have to fix these. There aren't even any residents in these up here."

"Damn, Trez owns these too? He needs to put lil sis on; I could use a job."

"Nah, he got you enrolled in school at the community college, so all you have to do is make the appointments." Stopping, she pointed to the black, ratchet ass Honda sitting on the curb. "That's your transportation. Bitch, you try me, and I will bury your ass now get out my shit!"

I rolled my eyes and got out. I only brought the bag of money and a bag of a few clothes. I was pissed that Tana did my ass like this, but I would come up. I went inside, and it smelled of mothballs and mildew. Covering my face, I saw she left cleaning supplies so that I could clean but she had me fucked up.

I got dressed and texted Mook my address. It was time that I started showing my sister just how much I loved her. She didn't deserve the life she had either with her ungrateful ass, and as soon as I had Amir's baby, Tay would be out, meaning I could cut off Tana without anybody stepping to me, not even Trez.

Chapter Fourteen

OMARI

Counting up what Mook and Tony took, I still didn't have enough of that nigga's bread. I was done using these dumb ass niggas, man. Here I was sitting in my brother's crib hiding out cause these niggas shot Trez. I didn't know them niggas was gonna pull up so quickly, and niggas knew the game so I mean it is what it is.

"Damn, so y'all only walked away with fifty, my nigga?" I asked, counting again to make sure I was accurate.

"Nah, we walked away with fifty-five, and this pussy whipped nigga gave Raya five for her info," Tony said, mugging Mook.

"Man, she did help, and I knew shorty could use it. Shit, you know she got Tana to get her ass to Charlotte though," Mook replied in his defense.

"So, she knows where them niggas are laying their heads?"

"Nah Tana put her up in some rundown apartment. She sent me the address, and I was gonna roll through."

"Man, this nigga. Mari, handle this nigga man cause he don't know," Tony said.

"He's right, Mook. Them niggas know it's y'all. It's a bounty out for y'all head too, dead or alive. You take ya ass over there, and they will have your ass. We in the Point right now, so we good. Lay low and let that bitch sweat. We done had it bro; it ain't worth it." I chuckled as Janet walked in without knocking.

"So you fucked Raya too, Mari?" she asked.

"Man, Janet, if you don't get your ass on. It's been a long ass day, and I don't have time for your bullshit."

"But you had time to make this baby. She's almost here now, Mari. When are you gonna hop off Tay's pussy and enjoy your family that YOU built?" she snapped back, and I lost it.

Jumping her face and grabbing her ponytail, I pulled her head back so tight to make sure she was looking at me. "Tay ain't got shit to do with this, and if you don't mind your fucking business, it won't be no family to speak on. I'll have my daughter, and you will be out there. It's that simple, now go!" I yelled, throwing her out the open door.

When it came to Janet, I had no worries. She knew when to amp and when to shut the fuck up. She put that front up cause the guys here, but they know what it is too. I wish one would try and step like Amir did, I won't be so nice then.

Amir didn't scare me at all. Just like him, my family came from money too. They took their shit, and I'll take mine. I wanted to work with Amir since my family had cut me off, but hearing that I was taking his traps, I knew I had caught their attention. My father has been at war with Amir Sr. since we were kids. I knew that taking his traps would show my dad how serious I was about taking over.

Getting Janet's keys, I walked out the house and hit the highway. I knew this was a long shot popping up on my dad, but I had to do what I had to do. My parents lived in South Carolina and if you let my mother tell it, who would come looking in bum ass South Carolina?

When I finally pulled up, the guards surrounded the Honda and checked the car. "All clear!" Domo, my dad's top security for the past thirty-five years, yelled and the gates opened.

I drove down the driveway and parked in the garage where my uncle was fixing up his old school Chevy.

"Wassup, Unk?" I walked up ready to dap him up, but he just looked up at me and shook his head.

"You tell me, young blood. I heard you out here reckless. Don't worry ya dad wants to hear it not me. I'm just the help, remember?" he said and went back to working on the car.

Shaking that shit off, I went inside and found my mother in the kitchen fussing out her young maid, Lucille. Lucille kept her head down but nodded towards me, and my mother turned to me. The scowl she wore hit me like a dagger to the heart. I lived to make them proud and no matter what I couldn't.

"Lucille, go tell Titus his son is here," she said, rolling her eyes and walking to the living room.

I simply followed her cause I knew if I didn't it would get worse. I wasn't the prize child, my brother Rique was, and they made sure I never forgot. I always come up too short or do too much, and they never see a nigga trying.

Rique was shot ten years ago, and since then they have been on me hard as fuck, grooming me to run their empire. Sometimes I feel like if they had another fucking kid, I wouldn't even be a thought on this here. Rique ran shit, and I looked up to my big bro, likewise. It wasn't shit I couldn't have when Rique walked this earth man, and the crazy part is Rique and Amir had a truce. A truce that both Amir Sr. and Titus respected, until one day Rique was hit up leaving a meeting with Amir Sr. and the shit had been war ever since.

Sitting across from both my mother and father, I was nervous as fuck. I couldn't look at either one, so I stared at the huge portrait hanging of them on the wall. "Omari, what have you been up to, son?" Titus sat forward and took a sip of his Scotch.

"Basically taking traps. Niggas stepped to me, dad. I had to do something, so he knew I wasn't no bitch," I countered

"You're that much of an ingrate that you use that language in front of your mother?" he peered at me.

"My apologies Ma, but dad, I need muscle. I need real help. I got bounties on my head. All this over Octavia, she is mine dad, you said so."

"I said she could be yours, but you couldn't control your anger, and you lost her to that bum. Now you ask my assistance after you act like a wild banshee in the streets. The same streets we will have one day?"

he rose up, sitting his glass on the table and walked to the full window that shows their lakefront.

"You will handle this as your final task Omari, and if you aren't fit, we have some else in line. You're dismissed." And with that, they both left the office and went to the lake.

Leaving out the house, I couldn't help the rage I felt inside. This was all mines, and they would not have the last laugh. Once I took out Amir and his empire, I would take out my parents and marry Octavia. These niggas should have stayed in line.

It was over with me being this laughing stock. Rique wouldn't have this shit, bruh. Cruising down the highway, I put in Soraya address, I was about to come out of hiding. If Amir wanted my head, I was about to give him the war he craved. I knew I could bring on some niggas who already don't fuck with him, but that would also piss off my folks, so I knew that was a go.

Heading towards Soraya's, I saw a pink Benz sitting out front. I parked a few cars down and waited to see who it was. Seconds later, Santana and Bella come out the apartment and Tana was trying to push a screaming Bella to the car. I saw Soraya come out, and I almost jumped out and blew it when I saw her stomach.

I ducked down when I saw then turning to come back my way and soon as I felt it was clear, I hopped out and ran up on the porch. Knocking on the door, I pulled out my gun and waited.

"Tana, I—" was all she got in before I pressed my shit to her forehead and pushed her into the house.

"Wassup, Raya?" I smirked watching her try and cover up her bulging stomach. Soraya had always been skinny as fuck, so this stomach was very noticeable. There was no covering that shit up.

"It's not yours Mari, and why you have that gun to my face?" she asked, walking away as if she wasn't scared at all.

"I just wanted to see your ass jump that's all. I saw your sis and Bella. What did they want?"

"Nothing but to see why I hadn't cleaned this dump up and to fuss like always, but the real question is what do you want?" she seductively asked walking towards me with a blunt lit. Raya was ratchet as fuck but had some of the best pussy known to man, and she didn't have any standards on holes.

"I mean what you tryna give a nigga? Ya girl is stressing me out and shit right here at the finishing line. Raya, I swear my daughter is going to always have, but I think I might have to let her go." I watched her push me on the couch and get between my legs. She pulled my dick out and began to lick around the head.

"Well, I guess you need me to relieve that stress, huh?" I nodded while she sucked and licked the head making a nigga toe curl and shit. "I got you, daddy."

She purred and swallowed a nigga whole. Grabbing the back of her head, I started forcing my shit down her throat, fucking her mouth fast and hard while she gagged and threw her arms up. I pulled her head up and got up.

"Take that robe off, Raya," I commanded, and she did as told. I bent her over the couch and rammed my dick into her pussy, never missing a beat.

"Shiiiiiiiiit, Mariii! Riiight there!" She gyrated back with me, and I knew she was loving this shit. That's why niggas loved Soraya's pussy. The bitch liked rough sex and could take the shit no problem.

Her pussy was so wet and gushy, and I was about to nut. She threw an arch in her back, and I sped up. Just when I was about to let go, I pulled out and let my nut go on her ass. She sat up straight looking like she wanted to kill a nigga. "What?" I asked, getting up and heading for the door.

"Look, Mari. They only hit me with five thousand, wassup? I need more than that."

"You got something. I'll have Mook come through with something, iight."

With that, I walked out the door and back to the car. On the way out, I saw a 'For Rent' sign and knew they weren't ready for what I was about to bring to the table.

ૢ&

I got home around midnight, and I knew Janet was about to go off.

When I walked in the house was dark, but I heard the TV on in the back room. Turning the kitchen light on, I had to jump back cause about sixteen roaches ran in all directions on the walls and countertops. They were just everywhere.

"Janet! Get cho ass up and come clean this shit up." I yelled to the back.

"Damn Omari, hello to you too at fucking midnight," she groggily said, walking into the kitchen like the shit didn't faze her. I watched as she let the water run over everything and put it in the dish drainer. "Happy now?" she said, walking back to the room and slamming the door.

Picking my keys up, I walked right back out that door. That's one thing I didn't understand. How could you want to take someone man but can't keep him? Janet just wanted the title and didn't want to work for shit. Here I was about to go to war, and my house can't get a simple cleaning.

Riding in my car, my mind went to Octavia. I felt bad for what I did, but when she didn't go to the police about it, I knew then that my baby loved me. Amir's got her brainwashed thinking he can give her the world, yet he still has to get with his dad to get work. She thinks that this nigga is this big baller, and he's still living off his daddy just like me.

I pulled into a motel parking lot and went to the trunk to get some cash out. After paying for a week in the room, I went and took a much-needed shower. I ordered some food and started mapping out my plan. Amir was going to come for my niggas hard knowing it was Mook and Tony who shot Trez, but it's all good cause I know a few Jamaicans who want his head as well.

I laid down thinking about how life was about to get better for a nigga. They may think they won for now, but I had plans for they ass.

Chapter Fifteen

BRAYLEN "BLEEK" WRIGHT

It had been two months since Trez got shot and our niggas still hadn't brought us Omari's bitch ass or his lil friends. Santana has been on ten since the shit happened and Trez stays trying to keep her calm. Amir and I have been running back and forth looking for his ass, and I was ready to call in some help. Bella has been bugging about us being gone, and I just wanted to find this nigga so that I could keep my word to Bella.

Kimbella had been blowing my phone up since I had left this morning, and I didn't have time for her mouth. I had been sitting outside of this damn doctor's office waiting for Janet to walk her ass out. I was just about to answer my phone when the office door opened. I had to do a double take because I could have sworn I was seeing shit.

I watched them get into the car and pull off. Turning my car on, I trailed behind them calling Amir so that he knew my location. We drove around to High Point, and they parked the car. I waited until they went in and called Amir again to make sure he was on the way.

"Are you sure that's her? And if they in High Point that means we found Mari's bitch ass too." I kept looking around to see if I could see any movement in the house. "Look, I'm right here. Just wait for me so that we can handle this shit." He hung up, and I went inside my secret compartment in my car and pulled out my gun.

When I saw Amir creeping up, I slid out my car and went to the door. I knocked, and when the door opened, I punched Ava dead in the mouth, pushed my way in, and saw that Amir was bringing Janet out from the kitchen. I picked Ava up and threw her on the couch.

"Chill, Bleek. What the fuck is this, Ava?" Amir said with his gun trained on Janet.

"Bleek, I promise you I tried to tell you, but I couldn't get in contact with you," Ava cried.

I had nothing to say to this girl. Here I thought I had paid for an abortion and looking around I had paid for baby shit. Ava knew I ain't with having baby mommas running around lifestyle, I had different plans for myself than multiple families.

"So fuck how I feel, and if I was ready, you gonna do you regardless, huh?" I said, pointing my gun in her neck. I swear all of me wanted to pull the trigger on her ass, but we weren't here for that. Shit, it was business first.

"Man, fuck this shit. Where ya mans at, Janet? And don't give me that rah rah shit about you don't know cause somebody is keeping you laced, and I know I ain't supply that for his bum ass," Amir asked, but Janet wasn't budging.

"Bitch, tell them before they kill me and my baby cause you wanted to act tough!" Ava screamed while tears flowed down her caramel cheeks.

"Hell no, I ain't telling y'all shit! You got beef with Mari, not me, so do what you gotta do," Janet said with her eyes trained on Amir. This bitch had a death wish cause he was about to pull that trigger.

"See obviously Omari done told you some bull to keep you thinking he's like that, but he ain't. Ask yourself this..." he started and cocked his gun. "Why would a nigga with so much power go on and hideout, huh? I mean if he knows he can handle me, why he ain't put me down yet, huh? Not only that ma, but he's making you hit every doctor's appointment alone meaning he's too afraid to check on his seed. I mean shit, if he doesn't care fuck it, you ain't my bitch." With that Amir pulled the trigger and blew her head out.

Ava dropped to the floor crying, and I didn't know what to do. I looked up at Amir, and he walked over to Ava and lifted her up. "You know where that nigga lays his head?" She nodded and cried even harder.

"What's the move Amir, you know that's my seed in there, right?" I said, meaning every word. No, I wasn't ready for kids, but it looked like she was due any day now, and I wanted to be there for the kid.

"Nigga, Bella is gonna kill your ass. I got tickets on that ass whooping nigga, you handle that after we get to Omari's bitch ass," he said and picked up the phone to have a cleanup crew come out.

"I can show you where I pick Janet up from, and that's it, Bleek. I swear I think he's gone cause she came here to tell me why they haven't spoken in days," Ava spoke up.

"So that nigga left her ass to hideout?" Amir laughed, shaking his head.

"Ava, let's go. You can't stay here. I'll get you a room, and if you so much as call and act like you leaving, my nigga will find you," I said in the coldest voice I could muster. I had bigger fish to fry, and I meant that shit. Kimbella was about to leave a nigga, and I don't know what I would do without baby girl.

After getting Ava settled in the room, I headed home for the night. I didn't want Bella up my ass, and I really wanted to talk to her about this shit. I knew this was going to break her heart and that's the last thing I wanted.

Halfway to the house, my phone started ringing, and it was the nursing home where we had James, Bella's dad, staying.

"Hello?"

"Yes, Mr. Wright. This is Danica from Liberty Nursing and Assisted Living Center. We have a problem here, and we need you or your wife to come as soon as possible."

"Is everything okay? Have you spoke with my wife, never mind I am on my way right now?" I said and hung up. I knew I should have called Bella, but I didn't want her to worry about her dad. I had things under control, and I just wanted her to sit back, relax, and work on school. Taking the next exit, I sped to the nursing home.

Walking up to the door I tried to pull it, and this bitch was locked,

I knocked on the door and then hit the buzzer. "Yes, I was called about my father-in-law. I'm Braylen Wright."

The door beeped and unlocked, so I walked in, and it was pandemonium. Nurses were running everywhere, and the director had pigs in her office.

"Hi, Mr. Wright."

I turned to see Danica standing behind me smiling, looking me up and down. "Yeah, what's up with my pops?"

"He left this morning, and we can't find him. I am very sorry, but I am doing everything in my power to find him," she stated, walking to her desk, picking up his folder and giving it to me.

"What's all this?" I asked, reading over his files and information.

"This is what we know about Mr. James from what your wife and his medical records indicate. Do you know anywhere he would just go to get away without telling us?" she asked, smiling at me.

"Yeah, I'll get my wife on top of this, and he will be back. I'll find him," I said and left out before them pigs knew I was here just the same as them.

I hopped in my car and sped off towards the house. I knew Bella was gonna tear me a new one, but I had to see if she knew where her pops would go if he wanted to leave. I told her ass he wouldn't like that shit, but nah, Bella knows best in her eyes and now look at us.

Pulling up to the house, I decided I would check and make sure Ava was still sitting like I said. Pulling out my phone, I called Tubbs.

"Yo?"

"Is she still sitting put?" I asked.

"Already. Food is on the way, so she's straight."

"Cool. I'll be in touch, Tubbs."

I hung up and walked into the house, I could smell some southern cooking popping off, so I put my stuff down and heard Bella singing her ass off in the kitchen. "Oh shit, Bleek. What the fuck?" She jumped when she turned and saw me.

"Damn baby, you can sing your ass off. Why you don't give me any shows, huh?" I asked, walking up behind her and kissing the back of her neck.

"If yo ass were here you would hear my sing plus more. Your girl is talented, but you got them streets entertaining you so you straight, right?" she said and moved from in front of me.

"Look speaking of I got a call today—"

"Kimbella, you really ain't giving yo daddy no beer? You are a trip. I'll get my own," James said, walking into the kitchen dining area. "Bleek, can you go pick an old man up a few beers? Kimbella acts like she doesn't love me no more."

"Nah James, you're in hot water. You done dipped on them bitches up there, so they're hurt. One said you promised to marry her ass when I got up there." I laughed, sitting across from him.

"What you mean dipped? Daddy, you said the director gave you cab fare to get here, and she knew you were coming here," Bella said, eyeing her daddy.

"And you said this nigga was straight, hmph a straight snitch. Bleek just told everything, and he broke the code. Why are you not up in his face?" I died laughing until Bella smacked the back of my head with the dish towel.

"Daddy, you can't just leave cause you don't like being there," she countered.

"I know, but it gets lonely over there, and you know I would rather be here with you and hopefully one day my grandbabies. I would say Bleek, but he the feds," James joked and got up.

"Baby, why don't he just move in. We have more than enough room, and I can hire a nurse to be here with him if he needs anything. I just know he hates that place, and I don't really like how they didn't find him until this evening. Anything could have happened to G, man," I expressed, looking Bella right in the eyes.

"Thank you, baby. I guess that's the only choice. If he isn't happy there then here is where he needs to be. I kind of feel better about it anyway. So, I made chicken and shrimp alfredo, fresh garlic puffs, your three-layer salad, and I also made you a steak cause I know how you like alfredo as a side, fat ass." Bella giggled and kissed me on the cheek.

I sat there and watched my baby prep the table and plates. I knew I should have spoken to her about it, but I couldn't risk losing her right now. Once I find Omari's bitch ass and sit him down, I know she will understand my motives.

Chapter Sixteen

OCTAVIA

It had been a crazy past few months for us all. Trez and Santana were having a baby girl, and I was more than ecstatic about having a niece. Mr. James moved in with Belle and Bleek, and they seem to be on the right track together. He might run out a few times, but only to get a drink and back home. I think his new nurse Ms. Patrice got him in good spirits cause I haven't seen him drinking in a while. He was always just smiling and laughing with her.

Even me and Amir were doing great. Christmas was coming up, and my mother and father both went away for the holiday. It didn't bother me once they explained they were working things out and their counselor was sending them away for a session with a great therapist. Amir invited me to dinner with his family, and it was all so new. We have been together for seven months, and I still hadn't met them simply because I always played it off.

Tonight was the night, and all I wanted to do was open our Christmas gifts under our black and gold tree and spend time together, but I knew this meant a lot to him. Getting myself together, I looked in the mirror in awe. I was laced in a gold wrap dress that stuck to every curve I owned. The open toe red pumps I slid my feet into complimented my slay since I had red rubies around my neck and wrist.

"You look amazing, O," Amir said from behind me.

"You sure? It's not too much or too thotish, right bae?" I asked, turning to see how it really looked.

"Baby, you look fine, amazing, and beautiful. I am one lucky man. Are you ready?"

"Babe, do you think they will like me? I mean I don't know how they felt about your other girlfriends, but I really want them to love me the way you love me," I said, applying a little lip gloss and eyeshadow since I wasn't a huge makeup fan.

"O, they're going to love your ass, especially my mother. My dad is tough only because of the business we are in. Trust me. If they get out of line, I will bring you home, and we will never go back I promise," he said and kissed my forehead. He took my head and led me to the car.

Pulling up to the house, I saw Bleek, Bella, Trez, and Santana all speaking to a beautiful young girl with long curly hair just like Tana. "Babe, who is she? She is gorgeous."

"That's Israel, my little sister, and thank you she gets it from big bro," he said, lifting his chin like he was cute.

Shit, who was I fooling. My baby was sexy as fuck. He had on all black suit with gold cuffs, and a gold and red tie. His locks weren't braided down, so they were wavy and flowed down his back.

"How old is she?" I asked cause little sis was stacked more than me.

"She is sixteen, and nah she ain't coming back with us or chilling at our spot. She is grown as fuck," he said loud enough to get everyone's attention.

"AMIR!" Israel screamed, running and jumping on Amir.

"Hey damn you ain't miss me. You just need something, huh?" Amir joked.

"Nah, I stay straight. You need me to hold something though?" she joked back. "And is this the Octavia I've heard about all day?" she asked, walking towards me arms open wide.

"That would be me. How are you?" I answered, smiling because she reminded me of myself.

"Girl bored as fuck with them old people in there. I'm ready to graduate so that I can be like y'all in school and loving my nigga." She beamed looking around at all of us. I noticed Amir had a smug look on his face when she said that.

"What nigga, Izzy?" he scolded.

"Son, guys, you made it, and this must be Octavia, Bella, and Santana. It's wonderful to meet you all. Come inside and let's eat, I know you all are cold out here. We might not get snow in North Carolina for Christmas, but we damn sure get these cold fronts," Isabelle said and hugged everyone. When she got to me, he smiled and hugged me a little longer. "You are more beautiful than he spoke of, Octavia. I need some of that glow you have!" She giggled.

"Yes ma'am, but I think I might taint the true beauty you conceal. It's nice to meet you, and you have a wonderful home."

We toured the mansion and finally settled at the table. We still hadn't seen Amir's father, and I was literally wiping my hand every five minutes from being so damn nervous. His mother was wonderful. She spoke so highly of her children and her husband, but I couldn't help but feel like I was being watched as she spoke.

"Amir Jr," I heard right behind my chair, and I froze. I mean I know my face had to have been purple because I stopped breathing, hearing his deep baritone voice boomed behind me.

"Yes, sir?" Amir stood, and he and his father both left the room. The large room went quiet, and I felt like everyone was looking at me.

"Well damn, he ain't never happy to see us, huh?" Bleek said, stuffing a biscuit in his mouth.

"Shut up, Bleek. That man doesn't have anything he needs to say to your ass." Kimbella nudged Bleek, and Isabelle started laughing.

"You are a firecracker, huh? Just what Braylen's goofy ass needs. You two seem to balance each other out with it though. And Trez why didn't I know you were a father-to-be?" Isabelle turned her attention to Santana and Trez.

"Ma, I thought Amir had told you. My bad," Trez said.

"Hmph, I see. So Santana, how has your pregnancy been thus far?"

"It's actually been amazing, I mean aside from being in the bathroom about half the day and not really wanting to eat, it's been great.

We're expecting a girl, and Trez doesn't want to help with the name." Tana side eyed Trez. She was in one of her moods, I see.

"A baby girl, that's a blessing, but don't expect too much from Trez. He is a provider, but when it comes to being soft, he ain't learn that yet." She laughed.

"Really, Ma? I am soft when I need to be, but shit most of the time I need niggas to know I ain't playing," Trez commented.

"Quantrez you better watch your mouth, that's what I do know. Go and get Amir and his father. It's time to eat. If he protests, tell him we starting without him, my grandbaby is hungry," she stated and began passing the plates around.

Amir, Trez, and Amir Sr. finally came back to the dining room and sat at the table. The looks on their faces seemed like things got heated, and I knew some shit must have popped off. I rubbed Amir's leg, and he looked at me and smiled. "I'm good, O. You, iight?" he asked.

"Yeah, I'm just making sure." I smiled, and when I looked up, his father was staring at me with this blank look on his face.

"So Octavia, where do you see yourself in the next five years?" Senior asked.

"Uh, I am not sure really. I want to see myself working in my career field, but it's not really my passion. I want to own various shelters and food kitchens and take care of people," I answered honestly.

"Hmmmm and do you see yourself having children, heirs for my son's empire?" he countered.

"If God sees fit, yes, but I also want to finish school and make sure my children want to be in this empire. I will not force my sons into something they don't aspire to be sir, no offense." I said and stood to leave. I don't know if he didn't like me, but the disrespect wouldn't happen.

"O, where you going? Don't be rude." Amir grabbed my arm, and I snatched it back.

"I'm going home Amir, and if you want this here to work then you would be right behind me," I said pissed that he wasn't on my side.

He rose from his seat and pulled me upstairs into the guest bedroom. "O, you're ready to leave and all my father asked was where your head was at? You basically jumped down this man throat for nothing!" Amir snapped.

"Babe, he's been looking at us all weird this whole time, and the first thing you ask me is about some damn kids? I'm only eighteen, Amir. I don't know about children right now, or in the next five years." I spoke my heart as my tears fell.

"Well, give him a chance, iight. I ain't saying kiss his ass, but just be respectful because it's not worth the argument."

I knew he was right. He kissed my forehead, and then we headed back to the dinner table. All eyes were on us as Amir pulled my chair out for me to sit.

"Before I sit at your table Mr. Amir, I would like to apologize for my actions earlier. You were just getting to know me, and I am sure you meant nothing by your questions except that."

"You may sit. Don't take me serious, Octavia. I just want grandchildren and Amir has been strict on that subject. I hoped you would change his mind. To be completely honest, you're the first girl he has brought home to meet us. You seem nice and quiet, from the stories I am told your ex wasn't close to my son's caliber." He sipped his drink staring at me.

"Omari was a coward who didn't see what he had. Amir, on the other hand, saw it before he even took a look. Your son does have a great thing, and I have you and your wife to thank for that. As far as children go, I do want children three boys and a girl if I had it my way. I just don't know if right now is the time to start," I finished, and he nodded.

Senior was a hard man to read, but I felt a little better about the situation now.

After eating dinner and opening presents, we all drove home, and everyone came to the house for a Christmas Kickback. I had gone upstairs to change since I was getting downstairs ready for everyone. When I came back down, everyone was sitting around talking shit about Trez's names that he came up with.

"Nigga, you not naming my niece no damn Bertha." Bella laughed, choking on the blunt she was smoking.

"Man fuck that, then what about Bonita?" Trez rubbed Tana's stomach.

"Babe, I'm half Chinese not Hispanic, why you playing? I know you really ain't feeling this, but damn try harder, boy!" Tana punched his arm, and he played hurt.

"What about Simone Unique?" I asked, sitting on Amir's lap as I took the blunt he had lit.

"Damn sis, I like that shit. Yeah, babe. I pick Simone Unique. O, you looked out."

"Trez, you lame as fuck, but Tay you're right. I love the name, and I know Maddison will like this one too," Tana said.

"O, I been thinking for a while about what you said to my pops back there. You're right, baby girl. Omari had something great, and he let it go like a coward. I don't wanna make that same mistake. Octavia Renee Mills, will you do me the honor of becoming my wife?" Amir said and sat a ring box in front of me.

I couldn't stop the tears from falling as I opened the box and saw the Cathedral Pave' diamond engagement ring he bought me. I loved this ring because it looked just like the ring my grandfather had bought my grandmother.

"Yes Amir, oh my gosh yes!" I screamed and kissed him so hard and so long that I forgot everybody was there, but fuck it, my man is making me his wife.

"Go, Tay. I am so happy for you, baby!" Bella jumped up and grabbed my hand to admire my ring.

"Damn Amir, now we gotta try and top this shit, and you couldn't even give us a fair warning, nigga?" Trez joked while he and Bleek dapped my fiancé up.

I couldn't believe this perfect moment. I didn't care about any other gift under this tree right now. All I knew was I was going to marry the man I loved. This just proved that he loves me back and that I can trust his word. The only thing in our way is my urge to still get at Omari. I know Amir's looking high and low for Omari, but I needed to find him myself.

Just as we were about to eat, Tana's phone went off, and she hopped up as best she could to get out the door. "Bae, what the fuck is going on? Why are you rushing out?" Trez jumped up after her, and we followed.

"Trez, we can talk about it later, but Soraya is going into labor, and I need to be there for my sister," was all she said, and I know I heard her wrong.

"How you going to drive all the way to Greensboro and get to her in time Tana and you got my seed while niggas are out here looking to break us? Nah, you lost it. Tell that girl to call y'all bum ass momma that's who got her, right? I got y'all, and I say y'all can't make it!" Trez boomed, stepping in Tana's face.

"Nigga, you got me all the way fucked up. Yes, this is your daughter and yes Santana carries her, but if you think you're about to tell me when I move, *ha-ha* you're wrong. Now I'll be with my sister. You are dead wrong for even trying to make me choose, Quantrez," she said and walked right out the door and left.

"Trez, I'll go with her okay, just chill. I don't know what my girl is thinking, but we got her," I said to Trez. "Babe, I'll call you soon as we get there I love you," I said, kissing Amir on the lips and running after Tana.

Chapter Seventeen

SORAYA

This bitch is telling me to breathe and relax, and I know that I can't. How you my blood my fucking twin sister and you bring the enemy to bring my child into the world? The bitch had the nerve to be laughing each time I screamed out in pain, but I knew I would have the last laugh.

"SHIIIIIITTTTTT!" I screamed as I felt the contractions stronger in my back and my ass. This shit was for the birds, and this was damn sure going to be my last baby out this pussy.

"You gotta breath, Raya. Ummm nurse, she's in pain. You need to check her cause they are closer, and she's feeling it with a damn epidural and shit." Tana jumped in the nurse's face, and she hurried for the doctor.

"Tana, chill before your niece comes out mean as fuck," Octavia joked.

"Ummm stay in your spot, and don't speak on my child. Thank you. AHHHHHHH!!! Tana, I gotta push. Bitch, get them muthafuckas in here, NOW!" I yelled cause it felt like I had the biggest shit stuck, and I needed to push. Shit, I couldn't stop pushing, it was like my body was pushing her out for me.

The doctors finally came in, and I delivered my baby girl at four pounds and 10 ounces. She was beautiful and looked just like her father. They cleaned her up and gave her to me and when Santana came and looked at her face that I couldn't read at all.

"What's her name?"

"Amirah Lee after her father, of course," I said, smirking at Octavia, and if looks could kill, I would be dead.

"Bitch, you wish Amir was your child's father. You should really get over the fact that he left you for me. You putting a baby on him ain't going to make him run back to you and fix shit either!"

She stormed out with Tana right behind her. Little did she know as soon as Amir found out about his daughter, he would run to our side and make sure we both are good. She's just mad cause I beat her to the punch, and knowing Tay, she's going straight to him with the shit and then she's going to leave. Ain't nobody stressing her mad ass.

Minutes later, Santana wobbled back into the room with an attitude. "Why would you do some shit like that? I thought Amir wasn't your child's father? Man, see Raya, you always on that bullshit and want me to save your ass," she fussed, but I just rolled my eyes.

"Tana, did you ever think I made that choice on my own, huh? Did it ever occur to you that maybe Amir's been lying to your girl? Yes, I lied to get my daughter and me out of a situation, not for a come up," I lied. "But since you obviously feel some type of way, leave. We're good, and we will get home," I said and turned over. My focus was getting Amir here, and she was a part of doing just that.

"If that's how you feel, cool. Don't call me for shit and as a matter of fact, you figure out where home is cause that apartment is gone. Bye, Raya." With that, she left out the room, and I didn't give a rat's ass.

My sister was always looking down on me, and I hated that she felt like she was better than me. In the end, I had Amir's daughter, so I knew no harm would come to me. And if she took the apartment, oh well. Amir wasn't going to let his daughter stay out in the cold. Fuck Santana and fuck Tay. They both will soon be distant memories.

Chapter Eighteen

AMIR

"Just make sure them are drops good. The last re-up niggas were sloppy, and we better not have them same fucking problems!" I boomed across the warehouse. We were having a meeting since our shipment just came in. The last thing I needed was my product to come up missing behind Omari and his weak ass team.

"Man, Amir, no disrespect, but I have mouths to feed, my G. I know this is business, so I got you, but can I at least get part of my cut so that I can get my daughter's asthma meds?" Ty one of my little soldiers spoke up.

"Nah, until I figure out who took my shit and the niggas that assisted him, ain't nobody getting shit, iight?" I looked around to see if anybody objected. Satisfied, I dismissed everyone and asked Trez and Bleek to hold Ty for a minute and his boy Que.

"Wassup, boss man?" Ty asked, rubbing his face with his hands.

"I got baby girl meds, man. Don't sweat that shit. I know y'all are good on my end, but somebody is helping niggas rob me, and that shit won't fly. Go pick up her meds and hit me up if she needs anything else." I dapped him up and turned to Que.

"Aye man, I'm straight. My seeds are good," Que said before I could even speak. I nodded and looked at Bleek.

POP!

"Damn, what the fuck, yo?" Ty jumped to the side, wiping his face and looking around.

"He was the only nigga straight out here, and the only nigga still eating, Ty. Your homeboy was getting paid, but he wasn't helping. He was keeping the shit to himself on who though. Look, I got a job for you I need you to handle, iight." I spoke to the guys for a while and then rode out with Trez.

"Man, you heard from Tana today?" I asked, rolling a blunt while we cruised.

"Yeah, Tana came home late last night. Why you ask, ain't Tay home?" he questioned.

"Nah, I thought they had to stay overnight. I got a text saying she would be staying overnight, and I've been blowing up her line, and she's not picking up. Aye, call Tana and see what's up."

He called Tana, and from his body language, she wasn't saying anything good. "Iight bae, we're on the way there now."

"What's up, nigga?"

"Man, let's just get to the house. You are in deep shit, my G." He laughed, and I knew Tay's overdramatic ass was about to dig me a new one.

Pulling up to Trez's crib, I didn't see O's car, so I walked in behind him to find Santana on the couch with her phone to her ear.

"Okay well, Trez just got here, so I have to go. Keep in touch please, I love you." She hung up and looked at me with the evilest eyes I have ever seen.

"Damn, what I do Tana? You looking at me like you wanna kill me," I joked.

"Nigga, you really fucked my sister and lied to Tay, huh? Here I was telling her she's wrong and that Raya's good for the shit, and you done did it."

"Man, ain't nobody fucked Raya's hoe ass. She tried, but a nigga pulled out when I woke up and seen it was her. Either way, I already told Tay about that, so why is she being dramatic?"

"Because that pull-out resulted in a baby girl, nigga!" she screamed and pushed her phone up in my face.

Baby girl was beautiful and looked just like Israel and my mother. Thinking about it, I turned back to Tana. "Nah, that's not my baby, and if it is, I will be going to get her from that bitch!" I growled. I was sick of this shit with Raya and her mischievous ass ways.

"Amirah is yours, Amir. She looks just like. You know what, go to the hospital and take the test, Amir. If she is, I know you will do right, but you need to give Tay some space. She's fucked up for real," Tana said and went upstairs.

"Damn, G. How you hide that shit from me? Now shit is going to look like I knew and didn't say shit to Tana," Trez said, opening up a beer and passing me one.

"Nigga, I had no idea I promise, but I'm about to find out." I dapped him up and ran to the house, I looked around for O, but when I didn't see her car, I knew she wasn't home.

Going over the speed limit, I rushed to the hospital and asked for Soraya Lee's room, when I walked in she was asleep, but the baby wasn't in the room. Shaking her ass, I needed to get to the bottom of things.

"You finally came." She sat up smiling but wasn't shit happy about right now.

"So this what you on now, Raya? Planting babies on niggas?"

"Amir, I—"

"You know what I don't even want to hear it. Just call that nurse so we can get this DNA test going. If she's mine, I got HER. Your ass got thirty days to get a job, and if not, I will be taking my child." I didn't even wait for her poor ass response. I walked out the room just as the nurse was bringing the baby to the room.

"You must be dad," she said and brought the baby close enough for me to see.

I looked at the sleeping baby in awe. She had my curly hair and lips, but she mostly had my mother and sister's eyes. Big almond-shaped eyes that I knew she could see through me with, she would always know when it came to me.

"Maybe she is," I said just above a whisper. "How do I go about getting a DNA test done?"

"Well, just let us speak with her mother, and if she is okay with it, we can get it started right away." She tried to walk away, and I stopped her. Pulling out a wad of cash, I slipped a few in her pocket.

"What if we let her momma rest and you handle that for me?" I asked and licked my lips.

"I mean you can keep the cash, I got you. Come this way."

After finishing my test, I made sure the results would be sent to my house and hers. I didn't have time for her to fix this shit in any kind of way. Hopping in my car, I headed for the house. If Tay wanted space, she had it until I found her ass. I wasn't about to play these games, Tay was my wife-to-be, and I needed her.

Chapter Nineteen

KIMBELLA

"Fuck Bleek, right thereeeeeeeee!" I moaned as Bleek punished my spot.

"Hell yeah Bella, say my fucking name!" he groaned in my ear, making me cum hard as fuck.

Flipping me over and pushing my stomach on the bed, he slid in from behind and pulled my hair back. "I need you to cum one more time for daddy, okay?"

"Yesssss, daddy!" I screamed, and he sped up his pace.

"Now Bella, cum all over my dick!"

"FUCK, FUCK, FUCK, BLEEEEEEEEEEEEEK!" I screamed as I came all over Bleek and fell onto the bed. He fell beside me smiling like a kid in the candy store. "Fuck you, nigga." I laughed. He just knew he was the shit, and he really was. Who was I to flex?

"Bae, you taking them summer classes for real?" Bleek yelled from the bathroom as I got myself together.

"I mean I was really thinking about it. Don't get me wrong I know it's my first year, but what if I can finish early and start working."

He looked at me and just nodded. I knew he had something brewing in that big ole head of his. "What does that mean?"

"Bella, I am behind you a hundred percent. I just needed to know in case I planned something that's all." He kissed my forehead, and we both jumped in the shower. I had four classes today, and I prayed I could get through them.

Walking the campus of Johnson C. Smith, I loved my school. I just wished my girls were here to enjoy with me. I had met a few people, but the only one I actually talk to is Emerald. I met her in my biology class, and she has been a huge help, so I figured maybe she would chill with me and the girls tonight.

Pulling out my phone, I dialed Tay's number while I walked towards the science building.

"Hello?" she answered.

"Hey, love. I'm just checking on you. Did you make it to classes today?"

"Yeah, I made it, but I sure thought I seen Tubbs' ass parked outside. I know Amir's ass is out here, and I don't have time for his bullshit."

"Damn girl, if I didn't have this class I would come scoop you. You know what, fuck it. I'm on the way."

"No, Kimbella. I don't need you leaving classes for me and my problems. I'm walking out now, so whatever happens, happens." With that, she hung up just as Emerald walked up.

"Hey, chick. You finish your paper yet?" I asked Emerald who looked tired and frustrated all in one.

"Bitch, no. Niggas were up partying all fucking night, and I couldn't do shit, so I joined them, and now a bitch's assignment is finna be late as fuck," she ran off. This is one of the reasons I loved her ass. Emerald spoke fast and meant exactly what was said. "Then to top shit off, them niggas was lame and ran out of liquor by the time I got to my third drink." She rolled her eyes and pulled out her phone.

"Sooooo, the fuck are you gonna do in there cause you know professor ain't hearing that at all." I laughed, thinking of her bright ass up all night.

"I'll figure out something. Why are you all glowing and in a good mood?"

"Girl, my nigga has that effect on my ass." I laughed. "But look, my girls and I are going out tonight, and I wanted to know if you wanted to join us?"

"Hell yeah! What time are you going? I can meet y'all at your crib," she said still in her phone.

"I'll send you all the info cause we'll just be leaving. We ain't ever on time anywhere." I laughed and walked into class. I was seriously ready to get school out the way so that I could turn the fuck up. I deserved it, plus I wanted to make sure Tay was okay. I know Tana was going to be in a mood, so I made reservations at a restaurant so where we could still drink, and her ass could eat.

Looking myself over, I loved how my curves were looking in my red V-neck romper. Bleek had just bought me a butterfly necklace that I loved. It was laced with diamonds, and I liked how it was just enough. I applied some gloss and headed downstairs to find Bleek. When I got to the living room, I didn't see him, and when I walked towards the kitchen, I saw him outside on his phone. He saw me and quickly hung up and came in the back door.

"Who were you cursing out, bae?" I asked, grabbing a bottle of water and my keys from off the counter.

"Nobody. Where you say you're going again?" he asked, walking up on me and kissing my neck in the trace of the V. I closed my eyes and grabbed on to his locks.

"Uh-uh, you cannot answer my question with a question, nigga. Wassup, who was that?" I pushed him up off me and waited for my answer.

"Man, there you go. Bella, I'll be back. Just let me know you made it there safe, man." He turned, grabbed his keys, and was out.

I just rolled my eyes and fixed myself back up. I hit the alarm and headed out my house. Bleek stays sneaking on that damn phone, and I was far from dumb. This shit was about to get handled, and he ain't know how soon.

I pulled up at Santana's house while she was wobbling out. I swear when my niece gets here, it was going to be spoiling time. She had her phone to her ear, and I had to wonder if she was talking to Tay cause I haven't spoken to her since earlier, and I was getting worried.

"Okay. I will see you tomorrow, I promise. Love you too, night-night," Tana ended just as she slid into my car.

"Who was that, Maddison's spoiled ass?" I asked, chuckling at the thought of Maddison's begging Tana to come get her so that Trez's can spoil her rotten.

"Girl, yes. She knows she has a niece on the way, and just knows I will need her help. She says she has some baby stuff for me, girl." Tana giggled, knowing she meant the life-size baby doll clothes and shoes she got for Christmas.

"Well, I hope she comes see me. This time damn last time you had her we ain't even get to spend no time, and you know she's our little sister too, not just yours."

"Girl bye with your selfish ass. Have you spoke to Tay?"

"Nah, I thought you were on the phone with her. Shit, I was hoping you were. I spoke to her earlier at school, but not since then." I checked my phone and Emerald said she was pulling up to the restaurant. "My homegirl Emerald from school is meeting us up there, so please be nice."

Tana just rolled her eyes and got into her phone like always. I turned the music up and headed towards the restaurant.

ﺲ

When we pulled up, I noticed Emerald walking up to us and putting her phone away. "Hey, y'all." She waved, and I had to admit lil mama had some style. She sported a white and gold wrap dress and some white pumps with gold heels.

"Hey Emerald, this is Santana. Tana, this my girl Emerald I was telling you about." I nudged Tana to get her head out her phone.

"Hello. Now can we please go sit down. My feet hurt and your niece is kicking me like I ain't just feed her." She wobbled past us. We were taken to our seats, and we placed our orders.

"Has anyone spoke to Tay? She still ain't here, and I know I gave her all the info." I said, checking my phone to no avail.

"Girl, she's probably with her man or something." Emerald laughed, but me and Tana ain't see shit funny.

"Nah, I doubt that, and neither does that concern you," Tana said, looking dead at Emerald. "And at the end of the day what went down is wrong she ain't really been speaking to me since she walked out that hospital room," she finished and looked away.

"I know she's not mad at you, Tana. You didn't know that was his baby, did you?" I asked, peering at her. If Tana knew that shit, then she was just as fucked up as Soraya's sneaky ass.

"Bitch, no I didn't know. I mean I knew she was pregnant, but at the same time, who am I to ask her who her baby daddy was? Shit, Bella, I have my own current situation if you haven't noticed." She pointed to her stomach, and I just shook my head.

"The more you speak, the more you sound like your damn sister. It has to be your hormones, but you might wanna check that hissing for real." I started to gather my things. "If you really think you didn't need to ask after all that she spoke on as far as Amir and Octavia, then you just as dumb and ignorant as Soraya. Emerald, I'm gone. You enjoy your meal on me. Sorry about this, but I can't do this fake shit any longer.

I rushed out that restaurant, and to my house, I really couldn't believe what I had just heard from Santana. Through everything, we never held information from one another, and the fact that she felt she didn't need to speak on this situation has got me looking at her more so as a threat than a friend.

Pulling up to the house, I tried calling Tay, only to get the voicemail yet again. I was drained and just ready to lay under Bleek and forget this night even happened. Walking up to my front door, I was surprised when it opened up, and Bleek ran out the house with his phone to his ear.

"Hold up, hey baby what are you doing back so early?" he asked, looking around and adjusting his clothes. I looked him up and down then back at my house, removing the thought cause he wasn't that dumb.

"Shit went left with Santana, and I had to leave before I smacked her pregnant ass for talking crazy. Where are you going and why you keep looking—" I was cut off by a Honda pulling up and some bitch beeping the horn. "Oh nigga, you fucking thought."

He grabbed me before I could get to the ignorant bitch, and I had to turn and slap fire from his ass. "Bella, I ain't never laid hands on you, so I know you better keep yours off me, ain't shit going on, and I'll explain later, but right now I gotta go take her to the hospital."

"Do what you gotta do Braylen, we good." I turned and walked into the house not even slamming the door.

I cried my eyes out as I watched him help her out the car and the belly she carried for him. I knew this wasn't a family member or close friend. They had fucked, and that was his baby. Wiping my eyes, I left the window and started packing my bags. I didn't need to come between a family, and I didn't deserve to be held in the dark. With everything going on I didn't know what to do or who to trust. I just grabbed as much as possible and left my phone and iPad just in case he came looking.

Hopping inside my car, I tried Tay one more time with no results, cranked up, and pulled off.

Chapter Twenty

OCTAVIA

Sitting across from this nigga I was ready to hit his dumb ass. Amir really thought I was clueless to his bullshit, but I knew Tubbs was following me. I didn't mind it because I knew it made him feel better with Omari still ghost, but I didn't think he sent him to kidnap my ass. We had been sitting here for about twenty minutes now, and he was just staring at me, I had nothing to say to Amir so silent I would stay. Clearing his throat, he finally found his voice.

"O, you didn't even talk to me about this shit."

I rolled my eyes at his calmness. That shit wasn't even phasing me. "Amir, you knew you fucked her, and you knew you didn't wrap up, so I mean unless you're saying this girl trapped you, I don't have shit for you."

"Man, fuck all that. I told you we fucked. I kept shit straight with you from the jump—"

"Noooo nigga you kept shit straight AFTER Raya came to my job with her bullshit. That's your thing huh, Amir? You like for me to leave let you do you, and you jump back in my face like everything is okay?"

I rolled my eyes and shook my head. No matter what, Amir didn't get it. I didn't give a fuck she had his daughter, or that they fucked because like he said, we already spoke about that. I was hurt that he knew she was pregnant and walked around speaking up kids on my behalf.

"O, you holding on to that bullshit, and you know it. I've been home with you every night and that ain't enough. You see and speak to me twenty-four seven. I don't know when I honestly have time to cheat or hide shit, let alone a got damn baby, and you know that shit." He had jumped in my face, and I couldn't even hold the tears back.

"Amir, you don't get it. I sat through baby questions from your parents, and you asked me about kids that same night as well and have been for a while now. I finally get on board, and you already have a child out here that needs your attention."

"So since she had a baby before you, you just up and leave me is that what you're saying O cause I just ain't getting it."

"Amir, just take me back to my car, please. I no longer want to have this conversation with you." I wiped my eyes and looked away.

He ran upstairs, and I went to sit on the couch. When he came back down, he had his keys and two bags.

"You stay. I'll go. I told you this was your house I meant that. Just know that I will be coming home Octavia and we are going to fix this." He kissed my forehead and was out the door. I watched as he got in his car just as mine pulled up, and Tubbs' big ass got out.

I went and jumped in the shower all the while thinking about Amir and this situation. I didn't know if this baby was his and I know he was thinking the same thing. I really felt like why not come to me with some test results or proof that this bitch is lying because last time she was speaking some strong facts.

I got out the shower and got right into our California King bed, I checked my phone and saw that Bella had called me back to back, and I had one missed call from Santana. I had no plans on returning Santana phone call cause I was really in my feelings about her sister and the fact that she knew.

I spoke to Santana the day after everything happened, and she swore she didn't know a thing about the baby being Amir's. She claimed she asked and Soraya assured her that it wasn't Amir's baby. I didn't know what to believe, but until then I was keeping my guards up. I knew she hadn't been to see the baby, and I knew Trez wasn't really fucking with her like that, so she had been getting Maddison more to keep him speaking to her. I had the shake my head at how much Tana and Raya were more alike than they thought. Clearing her call, I dialed Bella back and didn't get an answer, so I plugged my phone up and rolled a blunt. The last few days had been crazy, but tomorrow I was back on my bullshit. Taking a pull from my blunt, I smoked and thought until I fell asleep.

❧

The sound of my TV on *SportsCenter* and pots and pans banging woke me up the next morning. I jumped up and grabbed my robe and ran downstairs.

"Amir, I thought I said spa—" I stopped dead in my tracks when I saw Trez and Bleek as well, sitting down all looking at me, except Bleek. "What's going on?" I asked, looking dead at Bleek.

"Tay, I done fucked up man," Bleek blurted out shaking his head and running his hands over his face.

"What you mean you done fucked up? Bleek, you ain't making sense," I asked, walking closer to him just in case this nigga fucked with Bella at all.

"Man, O, come here with your wild ass." Amir grabbed me and pulled me onto his lap.

"Look, Tay. This old chick I was messing with got pregnant before I started fucking with Kimbella, and I gave her the money for her to dead that bullshit, and I was running around and see her big as fuck. I knew I should have said something, but I knew she would have left man, and I was right."

"How could you not tell her anything? In fact like dumb ass right here, you felt like you could tell her something this important at your own pace cause it technically doesn't have shit to do with us, right?" I asked, looking around the room.

"Tell 'em sis with they dumb ass," Trez joked drinking his beer.

"I mean y'all say it doesn't have shit to do with us, but then y'all want us to play step-mommy of the year to children that has nothing to do with us, or that we knew nothing about until you felt the need.

See, you won't have the problem with Bella cause when she holds you down, she holds you down. Ain't no switching up. But, you have to respect her enough to be honest and upfront with her."

I shook my head and went to put some clothes on. Knowing Bella, I was about to pull up on her little runaway ass. Looking at myself in the mirror, I was proud of myself. I had dropped some inches, and I loved the way it fit me. Amir had a gym built into our home, and I use that thing daily. I wanted a flatter stomach, but I wanted a healthy shape.

After getting dressed, I headed out the door only to get stopped mid-way. "Where you going, Tay?" Bleek yelled, chasing me from the living room.

"To check on my friend, and no your stupid ass can come." I rolled my eyes and walked out the door. Bleek really missed my girl, but he fucked up royally, and I can't help him fix it. Hitting the highway, I made my way to Greensboro.

❧

I pulled up to Kimbella's old house and saw her on the porch smoking a blunt like she didn't have a care in the world. "Bitch, you couldn't just get a room in Charlotte you had to make me come find you down here, huh?" I joked, getting out the car, but she didn't even crack a smile.

"Tay, you didn't have to come down here. I know you have a lot going on yourself. Where have you been?" she asked with no emotion behind it.

"Amir basically kidnapped my ass and took me to the house to talk. I saw you had called me, but when I called back, I saw you had your phone disconnected. What's up, Bleek filled me in, but what's up with you?" I asked, taking the blunt and hitting a few times before passing it back.

"A whole fucking baby Tay, and I mean I know I ain't the most forgiving bitch, but this bitch was ready to pop, Tay." She looked at me with tears falling from her eyes. Her eyes were red and puffy, and I didn't know if it was from the weed, or if my girl had just cried as much as she possibly could.

"Is it his?" I asked, rubbing her back.

"The way homegirl pulled up to our house like she knew where to find him, and the way he jumped in the car and helped her to the other side, yeah that's his kid on the way," she said, and more tears cover the stains from the last set.

I just shook my head and stayed by her side. I knew exactly what she was feeling and as much as I want to tell her to fight for her man, I knew I wasn't going to fight for Amir. That's when it hit me. Bleek said he saw Janet with this female, meaning she could be sent by Omari to get close to us.

"Bella, we gotta get back home now and talk to the guys." I jumped up and looked down at her like she was crazy. "Girl, get your ass up!"

"Tay, I ain't sweating them, and I need my time just like you needed yours." She rolled her eyes and sat back.

"Bitch, he saw her with Janet, Omari 's baby momma Janet. Bella, that's too ironic if she pulled up to your crib. What if she's feeding him all this info so he can get to us before we get to him. He could be there right now, and Tana and Maddison are there."

Bella jumped up and ran into the house to get her things. I hopped in the car and tried calling Amir, but didn't get an answer. I went to close my car door and felt a pinch in my neck. Looking up, I was horrified to see Omari and Soraya standing over me. My body went limp, and I could see them moving me to the back seat and Soraya sitting in the front. I heard Bella walk to the car and get inside. "Tay, we gotta hurry—"

BOOM!

Mari hit her in the head with his gun, and she was out. I couldn't move anything, and then everything went black.

Chapter Twenty-One

AMIR

Tay had been gone longer than I expected, so I sent Tubbs to her GPS location. Yeah, a nigga had his girl on GPS at all times, so when she thinks she's running away, I know exactly where she is. Bleek had been back and forth to the hospital to get his mind off the fact that Bella really left his ass without even talking to him. Shit, I can't even tell my man how to fix it cause I was failing at all my attempts. I was currently waiting for the DNA test to come back on Amirah, but looking at her, I knew she was mine, and that would mean I would have to have a sit down with Soraya's ass as soon as possible.

I was on the way to Bleek's crib with some food when Tubbs called me. Hitting my Bluetooth button on my car radio, I answered his call keeping my eyes on the road. "Yeah?"

"Bossman, we got a problem, Mrs. Montee isn't with her vehicle, and it's been abandoned."

He kept talking, but nothing else registered in my mind. Just as he got done, I heard my phone beep, and it was my father. "Tubbs I'll get back with you keep an eye out and tell everybody to be on these streets hunting!" I clicked over.

"Sir?"

"I have something for you. I need you to come pick it up from the house, and your mother made you a gift as well so come by when you can, but don't take too long, we miss you, son," he said, and I nodded my head turning my car and heading for the highway.

"I will and see you guys soon. Sir, give mother my love," I replied, taking my phone out and texting Trez and Bleek 911 so that they could meet up with at my parents.

❦

Pulling up to my parents' house, I jumped out the car and rushed to the front door. As I was walking in, I heard Trez pull up, and I went to find my parents. Walking into their theater, I saw my mother rise from my father's lap and come hug me long and hard. As much as I was trying to be strong because I didn't know where O was, my mother gave me what I needed at the time.

"We're going to find her, son," she whispered into my ear.

"Yes, ma'am." I nodded and let her go and went to get what my father had for me. "Yes, sir?"

"This Omari kid has Octavia, and my men saw them grab her and her friend in Greensboro with the mother of your child," he said, looking at me with disappointment written all over his face.

"Sir, I didn't know anything about the child in question—" I started.

"Child in question? We don't make mistakes, Amir. We do our job, and we provide for our families. If this child is Montee blood then we shall take them in and provide for them both," he said standing and walking away.

"Sir that is not an option. The mother is not welcome and is not to be trusted," I said, walking after him. In no way do I plan to help Soraya out and make sure she was good. I was going to get full custody of Amirah and send her on her way.

"Well, that's the thing, son. She knows more than just Omari so we need to make sure she feels the family's real love so we can get what we need from her. Find them and bring her to me, as well as my grand-daughter. Your mother is pissed that you didn't let us know. We expected better from you."

I watched him walk away, and I shook my head. I would never do things his way, and he knew this, but I would never disrespect my father. I needed to get these results as soon as possible, but first I needed to get Tay back.

❧

We all pulled up to the spot where my father's men spotted them take the girls. We relieved his men and watched the house for a few.

"My nigga, I swear that nigga is mine for touching my girl brah. I don't give no fucks," Bleek said as he got his gun out and put his hoodie on.

"Nigga, we ain't killing Raya's ass. We need her for a little while longer remember, iight," I said, and we exited the car and headed for the house.

Bleek and Trez went around the back, and I heard them kick in the back door. Following their lead, I kicked in the front door and heard running upstairs and doors slam. I followed the sound of feet and kicked in the first door and found Mook holding Amirah.

"Nigga put her down." I aimed my gun right at his head cause I didn't plan on laying with these niggas.

He put Amirah down, and I shot him right in the shoulder. I heard something fall downstairs, and I dropped Mook and went to see what was going on.

"Man, this bitch really tried to offer pussy while this nigga's wife is laying there out of it. Man, I can't wait to lay her ass out sis-in-law and everything." Trez shook his head and said, staring at an unconscious Soraya.

"Amirah is upstairs. I ain't seen Tay man or Omari's bitch ass," I huffed, getting frustrated cause my father was sure he brought them both here. Bleek carried Bella to the car, and I went back to holla at Mook.

"Where did he go, Mook? I know he told you and you already know. You only have now to give me the truth." I said with my gun trained on his head.

"Man, I don't know shit. Man, he ain't tell us—" *PHEW!*

I sent him on to wherever he was meant to be. The nigga held that nigga down to the death, but that was the wrong nigga to side with. I looked in the other room and grabbed Amirah and dipped out. I made sure Trez took Raya to the spot and made her think she was in good hands and okay and even promised to bring the baby after she cleaned up and got settled.

Pulling up to my house, I picked a sleeping Amirah up and carried her into the house. Tana had gone and got some baby things before I had even gotten home, and I heard her upstairs doing her thing when I walked in.

Laying Amirah down on the bed, I laid down with her and just stared at her. She looked so much like me it was crazy. Her eyes, her lips, her ears, and her nose were all me. I stared for what felt like forever in awe of the beautiful child in front of me. Startling me, she beamed a smile for maybe a split second, and I knew she was mine. I had waited all this time to open the letter from the DNA testing, waiting to fix things with O so that we could open them together. No more secrets and no more lies, I planned to grow with O.

Thinking of O, I got up and took Amirah to Tana and grabbed my keys. Sitting in this house ain't going to find Octavia, and I needed to get to my baby bad. Hopping in my all black Tahoe, I headed for the spot to have a talk with Soraya's snake ass.

Chapter Twenty-Two

KIMBELLA

"For the last fucking time Bleek, I cannot remember what happened to Tay because we were not together. I heard her screaming, and that's it. I couldn't fucking get to her, Bleek. I couldn't do shit, okay!" I yelled and jumped up to run to the bathroom. Locking the door, I sank to the ground bawling like I knew for a fact Tay wasn't coming back.

The night was so horrid that I couldn't bring myself to tell Bleek what happened. I knew him knowing wouldn't help anything but frustrate him from thinking clearly. I cried and cried thinking of Tay laid out somewhere dead because I didn't get up and go help her. I mean I couldn't, but I could have tried harder and made a bigger attempt.

KNOCK, KNOCK!

"Kimbella, you cannot blame yourself when you were not in total control of yourself, Tay wouldn't want you to, and you know that. I know you wanna find her and so do I. You know that baby, so come on out and come lay with me okay?" Bleek said through the door.

Wiping my face, I stood to my feet and looked in the mirror staring at the girl I am today. I don't think I will ever remember the girl I was yesterday. Stepping out the bathroom, I stood in front of Bleek looking into his eyes, feeling his pain and frustration.

"I want to help find her Bleek, and I mean all the way in."

Grabbing me and sitting me on his lap facing him, he moved my hair from my face and just stared right back at me. I couldn't read his face, and I wanted him to know I was serious.

"Babe, you know I ain't having that. If anything happened to you, I don't know what I would do with myself. I know you want this nigga's head just like us, but you gotta let me handle it," Bleek spoke, and I wasn't hearing any of that bull he was spitting.

"Yeah, iight." I got up and heard my phone going off followed by Bleek's phone ringing as well. Running to my phone, it was Tana saying she was in labor at Amir's house and Trez was already there. I put some clothes on and ran out the door to Amir's house.

Bleek was right on my heels as I let myself into the house and found Trez holding Amirah and trying to talk Santana through her contractions. "Give her here, Trez. Y'all go ahead we will be right behind you once we locate Amir," I said, grabbing Amirah and taking out my phone to let Santana's father, Tamia, and Maddison know it was time.

"Amirah's got a bag on the stairs, and her car seat is by the door. Ahhhhhhhhhhh!" Tana let out an excruciating moan, and Trez scooped her up and was out the door. You could see the panic and fear all over his face, but he didn't say a word. He was keeping calm, and that's what Santana needed.

Bleek grabbed the bag and car seat and took them to the car, I locked up and set the alarm and was right behind them. We drove to the hospital in pure silence, except for Amirah's whines every now and then.

Pulling up to the hospital, we jumped out and ran to the waiting area and to our surprise Amir was already there, and he didn't look good. His eyes were puffy red, and his knuckles were busted up his clothes were dingy and he looked like sleep would take him at any moment.

"Hey, bro. We're here, and I got my niece. Go home and get some rest," I said, rubbing his back, but he moved.

"I'm good, man. I just wanna see my niece into this world so that I can find her aunt," he harshly said, and I got up to walk away. I knew he was going through it, but so were we, and him taking that out on me was a no go.

"You got it, Amir," I said, folding my arms and sitting back watching Bleek with Amirah.

He enjoyed playing with her I could tell, and I also saw how she would be getting her way a lot based on how googly-eyed he had become. I think it was cute and maybe one day we would have our own, thinking about it made me think of why I left Bleek in the first place.

"Get some practice since that's your new life now, huh?" I said, looking around the hospital to avoid looking at him.

"There it goes, the real Kimbella. We can talk about it later," he said, brushing it off.

"Why not now? I mean it's just us here who actually know what's going on."

"But it ain't the place like I said. You know what here," he said, passing Amirah to Amir and getting up. "You want to talk shit about something you have no clue about. You can do that by yourself. Amir, hit my line when my niece is born, and tell Tana and Trez I had to go." Looking at me one more time, he shook his head and left out the waiting room.

"You know you wrong right that man was just—" Amir started, and I had to whip my neck both ways to see who the fuck he was speaking to.

"Amir, you worry about your shit, and I will handle mine. You good, remember?" I said, turning my attention to my phone and Facebook.

I swear I needed Tay here cause I was ready to bust Amir and Bleek in their faces and wouldn't give a fuck. The more I thought about it, the more upset I got, so grabbing my thing I left, I was going to find Tay's ass since Bleek needed space and him and Amir both think I couldn't.

Back at the house, I was dressed and just needed my final touches. Walking into Bleek's office, I went to his large portrait of Maya Angelou that hung over his desk. Pressing the side of the frame his guns, knives and other toys came sliding out the dressers. Taking my pick, I grabbed my bags and went to the garage and hopped in the beat-up Honda I bought off some girl for seven bands.

Driving around High Point, I looked at all the children at play and thought about what I had said to Bleek. I knew I had been petty, but I didn't think about the fact that maybe he wanted more for his children. Bleek may have made a mistake, but he showed where his heart was when he came and found me. It was just harder to let go the fact that I wouldn't be having his firstborn child.

Pulling up to my spot, I turned the car off and got myself ready to take down this motherfucker. I knew Mari had nowhere to go because his parents had cut his delusional ass off. I also heard him telling Soraya plenty of times about how when they get the last of Amir's stash spots they would lay low at his brother's condo. Pulling out Bleek's .9mm, I sat and waited for my time to go. Tay was coming home today.

Chapter Twenty-Three

QUANTREZ "TREZ" JONES

Watching Santana and Simone sleep made me feel like this is where I wanted to be for the long haul. Simone Unique Jones was born at 12:43 a.m. and has been a ball of light since she been here. My baby has her mother's eyes and lips, but she is me everywhere else. Her thick hair and long eyelashes and her bushy eyebrows, yeah that's all me right there.

I couldn't keep my eyes off them. As soon Simone started to stir in her sleep, I jumped up to get her before she woke her mother up, but Santana was looking like a pro already. Like clockwork, Santana got up and got the baby out the bassinet. I gave her two pillows and lifted her bed so she could sit up. Laying the pillows beside her, she held Simone in a football position, and I watched as she gently placed her nipple in Simone's mouth and baby girl went to work.

"Babe, why are you making that face? She ain't got teeth just yet?" I couldn't help but smile to hold back the laugh cause Tana looked like she was legit biting her ass or something.

"Baby, I heard that this shit hurts for the first few weeks, but that nurse didn't say it hurts this bad." She winced each time Simone would pull more milk from her breast.

"Well, we can always give her formula, babe. I told you that if this is too much—"

"It's not, Trez. I got it," she stated with much attitude.

"Iight, well I know my baby is hungry too. That's why you all in them moods, so let daddy know what you want to eat, and I got you," I said, kissing her forehead.

My grandma always told me when a woman was going through postpartum depression you need to give more than your all so that she knows it's going to be okay. I had my baby either way, and I needed her to know that postpartum or not.

"I want a Cook Out tray with an extra side of hush puppies, and fries with tea and a Reese's chocolate chip shake."

"I got you Tana believe that, and before I go, I want you to know just how proud I am of you." Dropping to one knee, I watched her cover her mouth and look at Simone latching her back on.

"Damn, I never knew watching my daughter come into this world would make me see life in a new perspective. You make me a better man, and I want to get out this shit I am in. I love you Santana, and when we get out of here, I want to do this ASAP. I need my daughter to have us both as long as she needs us as a team, not baby daddy and baby momma. Will you make me the happiest man, and her the luckiest girl, by becoming my wife and growing with me as her parent?"

Santana just cried and nodded which was enough for me. I knew she loved the kid and would hold me down and soon she will be even happier when we bring Tay ass home. Santana finished feeding the baby while I went to get her food. On the way there, I get a text from Amir with an address in High Point. I got Tana food and some things from our house and told her I had gotten some info from Amir, and I needed to see if that's where Tay was.

Chapter Twenty-Four

BLEEK

We all sitting here smoking a blunt and watching Bella's ass watch the house. I really wanted to know how she knew to come here and why because we cased out the houses on this street already and they weren't there. I knew this nigga wasn't that dumb. Bella was trying to get herself hurt for her pride.

"This is your girl so how do you wanna handle it?" Trez asked.

"Man, she wants in cool, but I don't wanna hear shit. We got her, and when we prove this nigga is not in there, she's going to know she needs to start listening to daddy," I joked but was pissed off at the same time.

"Man, I don't think she ready for this shit Bleek. I know you wanna teach her, but at the same time, you have to protect her," Amir added, passing me the blunt.

I knew what I was doing was risky, but I think Bella was ready. I had been taking her to the range like Amir and Trez had done for their women.

"She's good. Let's go pop up on her ass," I said, throwing the roach in the ashtray and hopping out the car. We hopped in the Honda Bella was in, and her face was priceless. "So you knew they were here?" I asked her calmly, looking at the house she had been scoping.

"Bleek, you didn't have shit to say back there, and right now I'm focused. So like you said, we can talk at home. It's go time," she said and placed her black hoodie over her head and hopped out the car.

We all followed her and then Amir and Trez both covered the back while Bella and I went to the front. I kicked the door down, and what we saw startled us both.

"It's just us, Tay," Bella said with tears in her eyes.

Tay was unrecognizable if you didn't know her like we did. Her eyes were both swollen and purple, her lips had been busted, and she was battered all over.

Turning her gun back on Omari, she looked at him with death written all over her face. "Babe, I got it," Amir said, coming from the back, but she wouldn't let up.

"You got this? No Amir, I got this. He didn't hurt you, he didn't take you, and he damn sure didn't rape you for hours until you passed out because your body just couldn't take it!" Tay screamed and hit Mari upside the head. "You thought you won, huh Mari? I don't care about the money or anything else taken, but my innocence and my pride that you can't give back." She emptied the clip into his ass and kept pulling the trigger like it would reload itself.

Amir grabbed the gun and threw it to me, Bella ran and hugged Tay, and Amir got them both out of the house and to the Honda Bella came in. "Call Will and Dre and have them at my crib by the time I get there," Amir ordered, and we followed through.

Running after Bella, I grabbed her arm and turned her around. "Bella, we really need to talk when we get home. I know Tay is just getting home so it can wait until later tonight, but we need to talk," I said and kissed her forehead and helped her into the car.

Getting in the truck with Amir, we lit another blunt and rode in silence until I spoke up. "Brah, where is your head at?" I asked, passing him the blunt.

"Man, I need to know where O's head is at. My nigga, I was scared as fuck of O's thug ass. She pulled that shit no hesitation. She didn't flinch or blink. She planned that shit, my nigga," he said, looking straight ahead.

"I feel you, man. Just don't say shit when you walk in the crib," Trez joked.

"Man I know, but I think baby girl is going to be good. I don't want her having nightmares and shit," Amir said, passing Trez the blunt.

"Man, I gotta talk to Bella about Ava and the baby man, like I can't keep her in the dark," I spoke honestly. I didn't want to lose Bella over no fling that meant nothing.

"Man, do what you have to do. Bella loves your ass, and she's going to hold you down, but you have to honest with her and treat her as your equal," Trez said, taking a few pulls from the blunt. "There is a certain type of way we have to handle our women because our lives call for long nights and bullshit. They're risking their freedom to be by our side, and they're holding it down as y'all can see. We gotta respect that," he finished and went back to the silence.

When we pulled up to the house, Amir ran in without even closing his damn door, Trez and I burst out laughing at this nigga, but both understood his urgency. Walking inside, Bella was downstairs holding Amirah and rocking her to sleep.

"Tay said she's good, so I guess we can go home and have that talk now." She stood and took the baby to her room.

Watching her with Amirah made me wonder how she would be with my son. I know it's going to be hard on her, but I wanted to see where she was at with it because Ava had been blowing me up about spending time with him.

When she came downstairs, she didn't say a word. She just went to the car and got inside. Shaking my head, I followed and got in as well. The short ride home was silent, and her being in her phone was just pissing me off. We got to the crib, and she stormed into the house slamming my car door. Her and this attitude were about to get her fucked up. I wanted to talk, but if this how she going to act, then I was good.

Stepping into the house, I saw Bella sitting on the couch with her phone in her face, and her legs crossed bouncing like she was mad. "KIMBELLA!" I barked.

"Oh nigga, you got me fucked up yelling and shit this way!" she shouted and jumped in my face.

"Bella, I ain't trying to put my hands on you, so I'm gonna need you to back up and speak like you got some sense."

"Nah, you should learn to speak to me, Bleek. You want me to talk to you like an adult, but you steady talking and barking at me like I'm a dog or kid," she said up in my face.

"You know what Bella, you're right. I've been real tight on you, but that's only because there is no room for error in my world," I said honestly. I needed her to know that each move she made and each word she spoke was being observed somehow and in some way.

"What do you mean, Braylen? I am still human, and I am going to make mistakes. You just have to be strong enough to either forgive me or move on from me. I love you, but I will not lose myself trying to fit your image because I don't expect that from you. I just want you to understand where I'm coming from." She quickly backed away from me, trying to wipe the tears I watch form in her eyes.

Watching her sit there crying hurt me as a man. I know I fucked up, and I know she didn't have one reason to stay yet that's all I wanted. Walking over to the couch, I sat beside her and rubbed my face, I didn't want to be the reason behind her tears, and I needed her to know where my head was at for her and me.

"Bella, I know I messed up by not telling you when I first found out about Ava being pregnant, but all this shit with Omari and then Tay leaving, I didn't know when was a good time."

"Braylen, a good time is anytime with me and you know that. I hate secrets, and I hold nothing back from you. As my man I want the same in return. If it will hurt me to know, then hurry up and rip the Band-Aid off. It will hurt much more the longer it lingers," she said, looking at me with love still in her eyes.

"Ava and I were just a fuck around Bella, before you and I even met. I stopped messing with her when she tried to lock me down, and I told her I didn't want the baby. I gave her the abortion money, and she assured me she had the shit done. While we were out following Janet, we saw them together. Look. I ain't saying what I did was right, but it's my kid, Kimbella. I gotta take care of him."

"You have a son?" She sniffled and looked up at me with a weak but genuine smile.

Smiling back, I said, "Yes, I have a son. His name is Brandon, and as fucked up as this situation is, I want you to meet him when you're ready."

She stood up and started pacing the living room floor. "Are you sure he is your son, Bleek?"

"The nigga looks just like me, Bella. Look, if we work this shit out then that's just it, I ain't fucking this up, I promise you that," I said, standing up and grabbing her face kissing her over and over.

I lifted her off her feet and carried her to our guest bedroom under the staircase. I laid her down gently on the bed and removed her clothes. She stared at me intensely anticipating the touch of my tongue on her body. I stood there admiring my girl, Bella wasn't green bean skinny, but she wasn't overweight either. Bella had this curvy shape and just enough for me to grab onto, but not more than a nigga like me could handle. Lifting her legs, I admired her pretty, well-shaved pussy. It was like she knew I was there because she was soaked already.

I couldn't hold myself back any longer, so I used my tongue to attack her clit. I sucked and bit on her lips, making her quiver and arch her back. She used her hands and forced my head further into her honey pot. I kept eating her box until she moaned my name out and came all over my mouth.

"Bleek, fuck me right now," she ordered, standing up and bending over showing her pretty pussy from behind.

"Yes ma'am," I answered and slowly slid inside her. "Fuck Bella!" I groaned as her pussy gripped my dick.

"I need to be fucked, bae. Fuck me, Bleek," Bella moaned, arching her back and gripping the sheets.

I sped up my pace and pounded the fuck out of her pussy. "Cum for me, Bella," I groaned in her ear as I used my thumb to play with her clit.

"Shiiiiiit!" she moaned and started throwing that ass back.

She gripped my dick with her pussy while throwing it back at me. I couldn't hold my shit back any longer, so I sped up on her clit.

"I'm about to cum, Bleek. Don't fucking stop," she moaned, and she knew I wouldn't. Seconds later, she was coming and so was I.

I kissed Bella and looked into her eyes. "This is where I want to be, and you are who I want to grow with. Kimbella, I love you and only you. I hope you find it in your heart to forgive me and move through this with me," I said, meaning every word. I needed Bella more than she knew, and like it or not I wasn't letting go.

"Bleek, I want to grow with you too baby, and we will. Just please grant me some time. I'm not upset with you or anything, but I just need some time to adjust to you having a whole kid. I do want to meet him though," she said, looking up into my eyes. I smiled and bent down to kiss her softly.

"Cool. I'll holla at his moms in the morning, and we can set something up. Thank you, babe."

"No, we can holla at his momma. I don't need you going anywhere near her ass alone, no sir," she said, getting up and going to jump in the shower. I just shook my head. I reached for my phone and tried calling Ava, but it said her phone had been disconnected.

I texted Dre and had him go check on her and make sure she was good and went to jump in the shower with Bella. Messing with her freaky ass, we did more fucking than we did showering, and a nigga was dead tired. When we got out, I moisturized my baby girl down and laid her down in the bed.

"What movie you wanna fall asleep on tonight, babe?" Bella asked me to be funny.

"Ha-ha a nigga be tired. Iight and anything you pick." I laughed, checking for an update from Dre.

They gone boss house cleaned out. What's the next move? I beamed my phone and didn't give a fuck as it shattered against the wall.

"What the fuck Bleek, what's wrong?" Bella jumped up and came to stand in front of me.

"They're gone Bella— Ava and Brandon are gone," I said, looking up at her. I swear I couldn't catch a break, but Ava had me fucked up.

"Where could she have gone, and why would she leave after just having a baby?"

"Because I left right after he was born to find you, I never went back up there, but I made sure she had a way home, and he had shit that he might need. She's mad I came back to you, man!" I yelled, jumping up and moving around her.

"I know you aren't blaming me now, Bleek?" she said, pointing at herself

"Nah, look I'll be back. Don't wait up," I said and walked out the room. I didn't need this shit from Bella, and I didn't want to say the wrong thing and fuck up what was just fixed. I just needed to get to Amir and see if I could find my son.

Chapter Twenty-Five

KIMBELLA

B *EEP, BEEP, BEEP!*
       I grabbed the popcorn and slammed the microwave door close. Walking back into the theater room, I joined Emerald and Tay who were both smoking a blunt. "At this point, I don't know what Bleek wants or plans to do about his son, but that momma is a different story. He blames me, and I know he does, but why if she was just a fling," I said, sitting the popcorn down and taking the blunt from Emerald.

"Maybe she wasn't just a fling though, Kimbella. Now don't get me wrong I am so on your side, but at the end of the day, these niggas ain't shit, and you have to think for yourself sometimes. He would tell you it was just a fling for you to calm down and shut the fuck up, but in reality, he worried about her and his son," Emerald spoke up.

"Nah, not Bleek. If he says it's a fling, then it's a fling." Tay laughed. "I just don't see bro actually chasing after no girl and from what my fiancé says, she got around, so I wouldn't be surprised if the baby weren't really his."

"Right, that's the same shit I'm saying, but he said he knew for sure. My thing is where could this bitch be?" I said. I had been wracking my brain, but not knowing the girl made it basically impossible to figure out.

"Girl, they're going to find her ass. Rest assured our men don't play, Emerald, you better get you one," Tay said, and we toasted our shot glasses laughing.

"Oh, I have my eye on one in particular already. He is sexy as fuck but I ain't really been sweating him cause I just found out he had a baby not too long ago, so I deaded that shit," she said, looking into her phone and smiling.

"Mmhmm so who got you cheesing over there?" I asked, pouring another shot.

"Actually, that was my sister. She needs me to come over. She is also having man problems," she said, getting up and grabbing her keys.

"That sucks niggas really ain't shit, Bella," Tay slurred obviously feeling the Henny.

"Girl, okay. Well, I guess text me tomorrow Em, and let me know the moves for after class. I'm free until seven," I said, walking her out.

"Girl, she's cool as fuck. All them bitches at my school are fake and just want my nigga or his henchmen, hating ass hoes. Let's Face-Time Tana, bihhhh," Tay slurred some more and tried to run for her phone.

"Let her sleep with your drunk ass, bitch." I laughed.

"I ain't drunk yet, bitch. I am good. Find a movie we can watch or something damn, and where is—"

DING, DONG! DING, DONG!

"Girl, there go the food I know your ass was about to ask about," I said, rolling my eyes and going to the door. I turned on my porch light and opened the door only to find the cutest baby on the porch in his car seat with and note in his lap.

Since you want to play family man to that bitch, here is your son. Raise him nigga since she can't give you one.
-Ava

I hurried and grabbed the car seat and carried him into the theater room with Tay. She must have sobered up quick seeing Brandon sitting there crying his eyes out.

"What the fuck? Whose child is this and why is he soaking wet, Bella?" Tay said, jumping into mommy mode. Since she had been caring for Amirah, Tay had become a great stepmother.

"Bitch, Ava dropped him off on our porch, and Bleek is about to have a cow. Read this shit. I need to call his father," I said and dialed Bleek.

"Hey baby, I know you mad I left like—" he answered, but I cut his ass short.

"Nah babe, we have a problem. I need you to get here now, and bring the guys with you."

"What's wrong babe, you straight?" he asked

"Now, Braylen!" I yelled and hung up.

Taking Brandon from Tay, I took him upstairs and bathed him. Since the dumb bitch didn't leave any clothing items, I used the pampers I had here for Simone and one of her white onesies and went back to the theater room to find Tay. I found her in the living room with Bleek and Amir reading the note. When he looked up, his face went from rage to peace and joy. He looked like he was the happiest man in the world. I looked back at Brandon, and he was looking right back at me smiling.

"At least she left him in good hands, huh?" Bleek said, walking up and taking Brandon.

"She did. Have heard anything yet?" I asked.

"Nah and part of me doesn't want to even worry about it. He's got me, and he's got you, so he will be straight regardless," Bleek assured me and kissed me on the forehead.

"See bitch, you just like me," Tay said, walking out the door with a playful Amirah in her hands.

I watched them and couldn't help but wonder if I would have the same effect on Brandon. He was so cute and really did look just like Bleek's ass. I turned and watched as Bleek rocked him as he headed upstairs, I followed and watched as he laid him down on his chest and they both watched *WWE*. Maybe this was better than I thought, and it was sure easier than I thought.

"I think you have a bigger problem, Bleek," I said, getting beside them in the bed.

"What's that bae?"

"I'm attached to Brandon already, so that means you have to share him with me when I want you to as well," I said, rubbing Brandon's back as he dozed off to sleep.

"As long as he doesn't take all my loving and kisses, we good," he said, leaning up to get a kiss.

"I think he likes it here already. He's been quiet since he had that bath, but you know we are going to need to get him some stuff," I said, sliding over so he could lay the baby down.

"Damn, you right. He needs a crib, clothes, pampers. Shit!" he said, laying the baby down and jumping up.

"Bleek, where are you going this time of night to get any of that?" I asked still rubbing Brandon's back.

"Wal-Mart. The fuck? My son needs something tonight, so I ain't waiting." He put his joggers and jays on and ran out the house.

I laid there shaking my head and decided to find something else to watch. Brandon had finally fell asleep on me, and I wasn't even tired. Before long, Bleek was back with just about everything Brandon needed. We set up his room and finally laid down for bed.

Chapter Twenty-Six

SANTANA

I swear the past few months flew by fast, Simone had just turned six months old, and I was loving every minute of being her mother. Amir Sr. finally let Soraya out of hiding, but she had been staying here until she could get on her feet. I just knew it would bring a strain on me and the girls' relationship, but it didn't. I honestly think that Tay might have known about the whole plan because she doesn't speak on it.

I had just finished breakfast which was cheese eggs, bacon, buttery grits, and homemade biscuits. I started cleaning Simone's bottles when Soraya came into the kitchen in a sports bra and boy shorts underwear.

"Damn Soraya, can you cover up? Trez does live here," I said without even looking at her ass.

Since the whole baby situation, I was tired of her ass. She put me in a bad situation yet again, and I was done trying to pick sides. My girls have never asked me to pick sides, but Soraya loved to say I chose them, and yeah, I guess I have.

"What you mean now Tana, everything is covered. If he's looking then you need to fuss at his ass, not me. Simone is your child, not me, so focus on them bottles, not this fat ass," she said and went back to the junky ass guest bedroom she stayed in.

Turning the water off, I walked right behind her ass. Yeah, she was my sister, and I had done my job by taking her in twice if you want to be technical.

"Raya, you have to go, I don't know who the fuck you think I am, but you will never disrespect me in my damn house."

"Bitch, get out my room. Trez and Amir placed me here to keep tabs on me for YOUR sake, so they ain't going to kick me out. To think you would put your sister and niece out is fucked up though. I'm glad to know where your heart is at." She smacked her lips and put her headphones in her ear.

I had had enough of Soraya's mouth for the past few days. I didn't give a fuck what Amir and Trez needed. If they wanted to keep tabs, insert a damn GPS chip, but she had me fucked up. I walked over to her and slapped the shit out of her ass. The next thing I know we were fighting in the guest bedroom.

"WHAT THE FUCK?" we heard the boom from behind us, but I kept swinging.

All of a sudden, I was lifted off Soraya and was still trying to her. Amir walked in next, shaking his head with a grin on his forehead. "So you ain't done enough damage yet, huh?" he asked, yoking her up and throwing her towards the hallway.

"Amir, don't handle my sister like that!" I yelled around Trez. Yeah, I was mad and had just beat her ass, but no man was going to handle my sister like that in my face.

"Shut your dumb ass up in here fighting like our daughter ain't down the hall sleeping and shit."

"Trez, you and Amir brought her here. I didn't ask for her disrespectful ass." I pouted.

"We brought her here so his father wouldn't kill her dumb snake ass. If I had it my way, we would have been dressed in all black a long time ago. I don't care that you beat her ass, but not while my daughter sleeps in the next room."

"Sorry, I wasn't thinking. I was reacting. She needs to go though, Trez. I don't want any harm to come her way, but she can't live here."

"Well, set her up somewhere, but them bills are on her. I can pay up for a few months, but she has that time to find a job and stack her paper."

"Have you talked to Amir about letting her keep Amirah overnight yet?" Amir was feeling himself keeping my niece away from her mother.

"Why are you all of a sudden Team Soraya?" he asked with a raised brow.

"What you mean? That's my fucking sister. You can't even question that."

"I can when she has done everything in her power to hurt the ones you love. She helped kidnap and torture your best friends, and she had your niece around that shit. You over here defending a bitch that if the price were right, would sell you off to the highest bidder," he fumed now in my face.

"Trez, I know you heated, but at the end of the day that's my blood, and I have to hold her down to some extent. What if this was your sister?" I asked, regretting I even let it leave my mouth.

"Tana, just chill for me iight. We can find her somewhere to go in the morning and even enroll her in the community college if that makes you feel better. Just chill the fuck out in my house with my daughter," he said with his back to me and walked out the room.

I stood there looking dumb and defeated. On the one hand, I know I have to protect my sister, but I know she's just going to turn around and hurt me. Picking my face up, I walked back into the kitchen and started back to Simone's bottles until I found something to do with myself.

§.

Riding around the city, I decided I would just meet up with the girls since I haven't seen them in a while. I finally felt my body coming back, and I had to show that snap back was real. I had on a royal blue romper with my Retro 11s. Since I hadn't been taking care of my hair, I decided to throw it up into a messy bun. I was comfortable, and that's all that mattered.

Walking into the restaurant, I saw the girls and then my blood began to heat up. This bitch Emerald had been popping up since I had been recovering from having Simone. Something about baby girl just didn't feel right with me, and I wasn't about to act like we were cool.

"Heeeyyyyy!" I squealed, walking up to them both and giving hugs.

"Hey bitch, it's nice to finally see our friend," Bella said, sitting back down.

"Girl, Simone and this breastfeeding on demand ain't no joke. She whines, and I pull a boob out, but she ate so much the first few months I was barely able to pump," I said honestly. I loved breastfeeding, but I also wish I could have pumped more in the beginning so that I could be stacked up now.

"Girl, you are fine. We have all seem to have taken motherhood up nicely," Tay added, smiling from ear to ear.

"Wait what did I miss?" Emerald said, looking at both Tay and Bella.

"Well, we both have children staying with us. They aren't ours, but they feel like they are," Bella said also smiling from ear to ear.

"So Tana, I heard you showed your ass today with ole girl," Tay cleared her voice and placed her attention on me.

"Man Trez kills me, but yeah I jumped on MY sister in MY house for walking around half naked, even though I owe no explanation," I said, rolling my eyes. Everyone was tripping for real.

"I mean damn you flexing on me like I don't know the real you, Tana. I know what she did was rude, but Simone was there. What if she was able to walk in and see that shit? You gotta think, that's all we're saying," Tay said, grabbing my hand and smiling at me.

I couldn't even hold back the tears that I had been constantly blinking away. "Tay, you're right, but in the end, she has to go. Does that make me a horrible sister?"

"No, Tana. That's you keeping it real with her. I know I don't know shit about you or your situation, but sometimes family uses that title to keep a hold of you," Emerald said, and I really wanted to blank on her ass, but that was real.

"You know what that's it; she's gotta go. I know in the end that's what's best for her. By the way, Mrs. Montee, when can my niece spend the night with her mother? Y'all know I am there too so what's the issue?" I asked, turning back to Tay.

"Girl, that's all on Amir. I told his ass he was dead wrong for just taking Amirah. Don't get me wrong I love having her around. She keeps me on my toes and sane with school, but at the end of the day, she needs her mother."

"That's what I'm saying. Amir's getting big headed, and I know Raya real shiesty, but damn her give one night before she moves the fuck out," I joked, chuckling at myself a little.

They all agreed, and we chilled and ate and talked like we needed to. Emerald actually seems really cool. She told us all about herself and where she came from. She said her mother passed away in a fire when she was young, and they moved around a lot, so they couldn't find any immediate family to adopt her and her older sister. She finally found a family in Asheboro, and that's the family that they knew.

By the time we were done, it was time for me to get home and start on my dinner. Checking my phone, I saw that Trez texted me that he was on the way home with dinner. Smiling, I replied and put my phone away.

"Well lovely ladies of the south, I got a man at home waiting on me, and a beautiful daughter that needs her momma. So it's been real," I said, getting up to leave.

We said our goodbyes, and I started to walk out the restaurant. "Santana, slow down," I heard from behind me. Turning around, I saw Emerald walking up behind me.

"What's up?" I asked, giving her my attention.

"I know we got off on the wrong foot at first, and I just wanted to say thank you for letting me in today. Well, at least listening to what I had to say. I don't have many friends, and I love my sister, but I needed something new, so I hope we're good," she said with this innocent look on her face.

"Uh yeah, we're good, Emerald. You're cool. I hate things went like that for you when you were younger, but I hope things continue to look up for you. I have to go, Trez needs me," I said, shaking my phone and walking to my car.

I was ready to talk to Trez and make him understand that all I want is our happy home back. When Simone was first born that was the most peaceful moments, and I know he will think on it, but for tonight I wanted things to go back to how they used to be. Cruising down the highway, I got the brightest idea and knew that Tay and Bella would be down.

Chapter Twenty-Seven

EMERALD DAYE

*P*arking *my car outside of Concord Mills, I got out and made sure my ass looked fat, and my hair was just how I liked it— bone straight with a part down the middle. I looked around, and sure enough there he was walking into the mall. I started walking in as well, tailing him. I knew what stores he liked, and I knew he was a shoe head, so he was probably hitting up a shoe store. I decided on Finish Line and went to browse. I knew I didn't plan on picking anything up, but I had to look interested in my bait to catch.*

Finally just as planned, he walked in looking good as fuck. His fresh cut and suit was such a turn on. I walked around the store but closer to him. I walked past him and looked into his eyes. Got 'em! He licked his lips, and I looked away smiling and continued to browse the men's shoes.

"If you're gonna smile at me, next time speak," I heard from behind me.

"Oh, sorry, "I shyly said, looking from him back to the shoes.

"So what's your name?" he asked, flashing that billion-dollar smile.

"Emily and you?" I finally turned and gave him my full attention.

"Trez. Look, are you hungry? I would love to get to know you," he said, reaching out for my hand.

I blinked and realized that I had been playing the moment Trez and I met in my head over and over again. I looked up and saw him still playing his game in his basketball shorts, showing off his sculpted chest.

"I didn't think you would still be here, babe. You always get up and leave."

"Nah, I just ain't got shit to do today. My baby momma's got our daughter, and I figured I needed to spend some time with you," he said putting the controller down and pulling me onto his lap. He bit my already erect nipples through my shirt.

"Damn, I can't wait to meet little mama," I moaned, tilting my head back just as he stopped. I looked back at him confused.

"Nah, I don't know about that, man. Her momma ain't feeling that shit," he said, getting up and sitting me down on my couch.

"Well, I mean we are getting serious Trez, so I think it's time, I'm here to stay, so I expect some respect," I said, getting frustrated.

Trez has been fucking me for months now, and I didn't give a fuck about how Santana felt. She keeps fucking up running off at the mouth with him siding with Soraya and had recently even left to stay with her ass.

"It doesn't matter what the fuck we got going on. I gotta respect her first. Now, I know this means a lot to you, so I'll think about it, iight?" he said, putting his shirt on.

"Where are we going?" I asked, getting back up and heading upstairs to change.

"I got some shit to handle, so I'll catch you later. Look, I ain't mad or anything it's just hard for to even get Simone alone right now, Emily. I know you want to meet her so how about this. Her birthday is coming up, so maybe you can meet her and her mother then?" he said, kissing my forehead as I nodded. I watched him leave, and once he was out of sight, I jumped around screaming.

I knew this was going to blow their minds seeing me walk into the party with Trez. Since the fight Tana and Soraya had, their relationship went downhill, I took that as my cue to step in for Trez's sake. They argued, fussed, and fought, and he would run to me and tell it. Tana used to as well, but I conveniently departed from the circle for a while. In no time Trez had moved out and left her and Simone the house and got himself a studio apartment.

On top of everything going on, Tana never returned to school. When I say she fell off, she let herself go. There wasn't much I had to do to get Trez to notice me because I stay on my shit. I wasn't dumb, and I knew what I was doing was wrong, but I also fell for Trez. When I first baited him, I'll say it was for the wrong reasons. But now, I had true feelings for him, and I wouldn't be giving him up easily. I got my book bag ready and grabbed my keys when my phone started to vibrate. Stopping dead in my tracks, I answered the unknown number.

"Hello?"

"Meet up now and don't keep me waiting." And they hung up.

Shaking my head, I locked up and jumped in my car. I was tired of this shit, and I couldn't wait until this whole thing was over so that I could go back to being happy.

Chapter Twenty-Eight

TREZ

Today was Simone's six months birthday party, and a nigga was hype as hell. This past few months had been trying, but I was finally back to be happy and chilling with Emily. It's crazy how much she chill and lets me work. I mean she doesn't know what I do yet, but I want to keep it this way. Tana and I ain't been seeing eye to eye, and I recently moved out from our house we shared. It hurt me to have to leave, but I knew I would still be there for them both.

I just got tired of picking up after Santana messes. She was an amazing mother and wonderful girlfriend, but at the end of the day, I wanted her to have her own thing— a hobby or job or career like she always spoke about. I promised Tana that I would support her getting school done and taking care of Simone and I did my part. I found out this whole time I was thinking she was at school or at least in the process of enrolling, she hadn't been enrolled since we found out she was pregnant with Simone.

I couldn't trust her ass anymore, so she had to go. I loved her with all of me still though. I couldn't shake Tana, and one day I hoped I would be able to commit fully to Emily, but right now I had to get myself together.

Making sure I was fresh, I stood up just as Emily was walking out from her room. Baby girl was beautiful and the way her ass sat in her Fashion Nova jeans, had me saying the first thing that popped into my head.

"Damn!"

"What's wrong, too much for the party? Ugh, I thought you would say that. I'll go change, babe," she said and began to turn around for the bedroom.

"Nah, nah, nah, you good, Em. You look damn good, babe. Let's go. I don't wanna be late," I said, kissing her on her lips.

She stuck her tongue in my mouth, and my mans rocked up. She knew what she was doing cause the next thing I knew, she was deep throating the shit out of my dick.

After a quick session, we were finally pulling up to the party. The way Tana had decorated the house even outside was amazing. My baby was great at that, and I knew if she put her mind to it, she could design houses. "This is amazing, Trez," Emily said, looking at the house in awe.

"Yeah, come on. I want you to meet everyone," I said, helping her out the car and walking up the stairs to the house.

When we walked in, it was like all eyes were on us, and Tay and Bella mainly looked like they wanted to bury Emily where she stood. I knew it was going to be a stare down, but these females looked like they just might handle this shit at my baby's party, and it wasn't going to happen.

"Well damn, hey to y'all too. Where are Tana and Simone?" I asked, walking Emily through the house.

"I'm right here, Quantrez. Hello, Emerald." *Click!*

I looked up, and Tana had her gun trained on both me and Emily. Everybody froze, but I saw Amir appear from under the staircase. "Fuck you doing, Tana? Put that shit up," I calmly said as she descended down.

"Nigga, you really don't know who you fucking with huh?" she said, putting the gun right on Emily who was shaking beside me.

"Santana, I don't know what has gotten into you, but you put that shit up! This is not you, baby girl, and you are scaring your sister!" Mike, her father, said, covered a crying Maddison's eyes.

I looked back at Tana, and she dropped the gun. I rushed to take it and gave it to Amir while Bleek carried Tana away.

"Emerald, I will catch your ass, and my baby daddy won't be able to save you hoe!" Tana yelled and kicked as Bleek pulled her into the guest bedroom.

"The fuck wrong with you, Emerald?" Tay asked but before she could get anything out, Bella had jump clean on her and started beating Emily's ass. I was so confused I didn't know what the fuck was going on, and why did they keep calling Emily Emerald.

"Bella, chill!" I heard and came back to reality.

Grabbing Emily, we left out the house and jumped in the car. The whole ride I didn't say shit to her, and she didn't say shit to me. I pulled up to her crib in record timing and hopped out not even waiting for her. Using my key, I went inside and paced until she graced the living room with her presence. "Trez, listen—" she started.

SLAP!

"Bitch, you really tried to play me huh? Emily, or is it Emerald? How you know my baby momma, bitch?" I asked, holding her by her hair. All that crying and pleading wasn't working for me, I was confused and stuck because I didn't want to be doing what I was doing. I really felt something for Emily, so this shit hurt a nigga.

"Trez, let me explain, pleaseeeee!" She cried harder.

Letting go of her hair, I watched her fall to the ground and continued to cry. "You better get to talking," I said and sat on the couch.

"My name is Emerald, and I only lied because I didn't think this would last. I didn't know Santana was your child's mother because she never said your name or your daughter's name ever. I swear I didn't know, Trez," she said, crawling to my lap and unzipping my pants. She licked the head of my dick, and I let my head fall back on the couch.

She sucked and slurped on my dick until I couldn't take it anymore. I grabbed the back of her head and began to pound my dick into her mouth. I don't know what got into me, but I was beating her throat up, taking all my frustration out on her mouth. One I felt myself about to cum, I let her have her way, and she swallowed my seeds gulp by gulp.

"I really mean it, Trez. I love you, and I know it will take some time to get your trust back, but at least let me try," she said, wiping her mouth and standing up.

"Nah, we good. Just don't ever cross me or lie to me again, Emerald. I gotta keep it real I'm feeling you too, but you gotta keep it a buck with me, iight?" I said, kissing her forehead.

I was still in my feelings about Simone's party, and I just wanted to take my shower and go get her the best make up gift ever.

Chapter Twenty-Nine

OCTAVIA

"Maybe he ain't fucking know, but either way, he's fucking another bitch and thought he could just bring her to my house. That nigga ain't right Tay, and if he brings her to the wedding I swear I'm going to lose it, and you are just going to have to be mad," Tana ranted.

"Bitch, okay. I can't believe I would bring this snake bitch around y'all. I am so sorry, Santana. You told us she was off and we didn't believe you," Bella said.

"Nah, it's all good. The truth always hit the light. She fed me all that advice and was fucking him this whole time."

"Damn, can y'all just chill for a minute please?" I yelled, turning around from the mirror.

I was finally at my last fitting for my wedding dress, and I didn't need the drama. We had been on this party drama for three weeks now, and Trez and the guys had been passed it. I had also spoken with Emerald, and she actually seemed like she really loved Trez. I felt for my girl, but she needed to move on cause chasing Trez was hurting her more than letting go ever would.

"Excuse me for having problems in my relationship. Not everyone can just find a great man and marry him. We don't all have fairy tale relationships," Tana said, rolling her eyes, and I was fed up with the shit.

"You know what, Tana. You got me fucked all the way up if you think you about to talk to me like I ain't been through some shit,' I said, getting off the podium and walking towards her.

She stood as well, but I wasn't on that, but I could be.

"Instead of you comparing yourself and your man to mine, how about to focus on yourself how you could change the situation. You're so focused on the that fact that he left and is now happy,that you can't see he was pushing your simple ass."

"Pushing me how, Tay? The nigga stayed in the streets and was hardly home with Simone and me. That nigga don't give a fuck, and if he did, he damn sure wouldn't be in another's bitch face. You over here defending him and this bitch, so make sure they're in your damn wedding. My sister was right about one thing. If it ain't about Tay, then shit just don't fucking matter," she said and gathered her things to leave.

"Make sure you stay gone then with your snake ass!" I yelled after her. I be damned if she was going to fuck up my day with her miserable ass.

"You ain't have to go in on her like that, Octavia," Bella said, shaking her head.

"What part was a lie though, Bella? She's so stuck on being this fairytale couple that she forgot when that nigga had a whole baby on me, or that he fucked her sister in general while still trying to build this relationship with me. Like no, I will not be made out as a bully. She needed to hear that shit, and she's just mad cause the shit hurt. Tana better let that shit sink in and make some changes for the better," I said, turning back around to look at my dress.

I love my mermaid style dress that was laced with diamonds. I was in love, and I knew Amir would shed a few when he finally saw me in my dress.

"I can't believe you about to get married on me, bitch." Bella walked up and hugged me from behind, supporting a pouty face.

"I know. It just doesn't feel real. I mean we have been through a lot of shit. There is something I wanted to talk to you about. It was going to be Tana, but maybe this is for the better," I said and motioned for the seamstress to leave the room.

"What's up, cause I feel like I might have to light a blunt in this dressing room?" Bella sat down and rolled her eyes.

"I want Amir to teach me the ropes before we say, 'I do'. I really want to be able to hold my man down. I need to be the queen to his kingdom. I know he's going to be extra hesitant, but I know how to convince him to give me my way. What do you think Bleek will say?" I asked, searching her face for any sign of a negative answer.

"Girl, he's going to curse me plum out and then tell me no. I mean trust me, I'm down, I have already gone down this road when all that shit popped off with Omari and Raya. He shut me down so quick Tay that I ain't never ask again. Don't get me wrong he takes me to the range weekly for just in case situation, but I want to know the operation so that if anything happens I can take my place."

"That's exactly what I was saying, girl. We can do this shit man, and I know they need our help just in case. I swear they act as if we're asking to take their spots now and shit." We both laughed.

"Girl, okay. So what are you going to do about this Santana thing?" she asked, looking up from her phone back at me.

I just shook my head and stared at myself in the mirror. I loved Santana, but the more things didn't go her way, the more she started to act like Mae and Soraya, and I didn't like that shit. The day of the party she not only put herself and child in harm's way, but Amirah and Brandon were both there as well.

"I really don't know Bella, but I just don't feel her the way that I used to, and that ain't good. I can't trust her, Bella," I said and gave my dress my attention. Today was about me, and I wanted my time.

Since taking on Amirah, I have been with her more than Amir. I knew this was going to be a huge responsibility so when I got his text to get home because something urgent came up, I didn't think anything of it. I was used to it by now, but I also saw that Amirah had a mother, and as much as I wish I were her, I wasn't. He spent time with her, but he needed to be around her more if he wanted to have sole custody.

I shook my head as I walked into my house and saw Amirah's toys everywhere outside of her playpen. I started picking them up one by one when I heard, "Mama" from in front of me. Looking up, I saw Amirah waddling full speed towards me with her hands held out. Picking her up I gave her kisses all over her face and tickled her. She squealed and giggled. I loved these moment, but I also felt her mother deserved that same treatment.

As much as I didn't like Soraya, this was her damn child and she needed to be here for when he needs to leave out at the last minute. Speaking of the devil, in walks Amir's sexy ass, and as mad as I was for having to leave my dress appointment early, all I wanted was to feel him at this moment.

"Hey, baby. Thank you for getting here in time. Do you need anything before I go?" he said, walking up and kissing mine and Amirah's forehead.

"Yeah, for you to take Toot to her mother. Why can't Soraya watch the child she carried? I love her, so don't start that bull about me not wanting to play my role cause I do that plus more. I just think her mother needs to step it up. You have her surrounded with security so that she doesn't do no crazy shit against you, but she can't keep your child during that time?" I said finally having enough. He just sat there and stared me down like he wanted to say something, but didn't want to argue.

"Look, O. I know you're tired, but you also know that's out. We have been through this. I don't trust that bitch around my daughter. If anything happened to her, I would never forgive myself, and you wouldn't either. If you need help around here, hire a nanny or start letting Ms. Patrice watch her like she asks. You're making things hard on yourself. I'll be right back and I'll send my mother to get her just give her a minute," he said and tried to walk away.

"Wait when did your mother come to town, Amir?" I yelled, trying to chase him with Amirah's big self in my arms.

"This morning. She was coming anyway. That's what came up, okay? Babe, I will be right back. My father doesn't like to be held waiting," he said and kissed me before hopping in his truck and peeling off.

I turned around and looked at the mess he left for me to clean. I couldn't even think of where I should start, and on top of everything, I didn't know when his mother would arrive. I sat Amirah in her crib and turned her TV to *Trolls*. I returned and started cleaning from top to bottom. It took me about two hours to get everything done as well as keep Amirah content at the same time.

Amirah finally fell asleep, so I jumped in the shower and got ready for Isabella to arrive. I hated when Amir would spring these moves on me at the last minute. I put my sandals on and went to get Amirah dressed just as the doorbell rang. Grabbing Amirah, I went to answer the door,

"Let's go see Granny."

"Oh my, look at her. Hello Octavia, how have you been sweetheart?" Isabelle said, walking in arms wide open reaching for Amirah who was hesitant to go to her at first.

"It's okay, princess. That is your grandmother," I heard come from behind Isabelle, and sure enough Amir and Senior were walking in right behind him.

"Hello Amir Sr., how are you?" I said, eying Amir for being so messy. Here I was his wife-to-be, and I looked like I was hitting a Cook Out or something.

"Peaceful now that you took care of a huge problem I was having. I am actually here on business. Is this my grandchild from the Lee twin, son?" he said, giving Amir his attention.

"This is your granddaughter Amirah, and yes Soraya is her mother, but I am working hard to get her rights revoked," Amir spoke up, and I wanted to know the importance of his questions.

I watched how interested Senior was with Amirah, and I didn't really like it. I know that's his granddaughter, but it looked as if he saw money signs when he stared at her.

"Son, looking at this child, you must do what's right and marry her mother. The Lee family line goes deeper than you think. Soraya and Santana's grandfather Tao Lee has an army of goons of his own, and they come in all shapes and sizes. His manpower could be beneficial to our cause. You marry his granddaughter, and we take over their family business with ease," he said at this point pacing the floor and talking to us all in the room.

No one said a word, and I only looked to Amir for answers. His father must be out his rabbit ass mind if he thought he was about to tell Amir who he would marry. Still, nothing was said.

"Amir, are you going to say something?" I said when he still hadn't found his voice.

"Amir, you cannot come into his home and make such grand request like this. These two are engaged to be married, and we can still have that empire, but you don't want to put the work in. I cannot believe you. Sorry, Octavia," Isabelle said, shaking her head, but I was more focused on Amir and how he looked at his father.

"Father, I have followed you hand and foot since I was a young dumb boy. You showed me the ropes and made me the man that I am, so you should feel and understand me when I say that I will marry Octavia this weekend, and I will raise Amirah together with my wife, Octavia. Mother, you can stay, and I will take you to the townhouse when you're ready. Tubbs, escort my father out of my house and off my land," Amir said so calmly and walked to his office. I looked to his mother, and she had tears streaming from her eyes.

"This man will start a war he cannot win with the Lee family for the sake of you. Can you live with the deaths of thousands for the love from one man out of a million? You will be a black widow," he said and walked out the house with Tubbs hot on his tracks.

I was about to go check on Amir when I felt his mother's hand on my shoulder.

"I truly am sorry, Octavia. I enjoy you and love how you look with my son. I support this wedding, and I just want you to know that things will be okay. Just give him time to adjust to you and get out of his customs." She weakly smiled, and yet all I saw was the stains from the tears she had just cried.

I nodded and left her with Amirah while I went to find Amir and see what the hell was going on. Approaching his large oak office doors, I contemplated how I wanted to handle this conversation. Opening the doors, I saw him staring at a picture of Amirah and me sleeping on her plush rug. It was his favorite picture of us because it was the first time we had really got to bond and she had finally gotten used to being with just me. I walked around his desk and rubbed my fingers through his locs, bending over to kiss his forehead.

"Amir, talk to me," I whispered.

"O, things are about to get real, I don't want to keep you in the dark, but that's the only way to keep you safe. My father was right, the Lee Family is nobody to play with, and I've seen them do gruesome shit to kids, man. Look, we might have to handle some real shit, so you and the girls might need to go away for a while," he said, and I had to step back because I know I heard wrong.

"But they would never hurt Amirah; that's their blood too, Amir." This shit wasn't making an ounce of sense, and I was really lost.

"Look when Mae chose to be with Mike, Tao disowned her ass, and that meant Soraya and Santana and so forth. Look at their track record. You never met Tana's other family, have you?" he asked, looking up at me.

Thinking back, I really haven't met her other side, but there was an aunt that Tana said her mother would always call, and she would send her mother money.

"Nah, I figured something like that, but not so extreme as mob shit. Where are you sending us and when are we leaving Amir? What about my parents, and you staying here?"

He rose from the chair and grabbed my face gently lifting it so that he could look me in my eyes.

"O, I have to do this to keep you and my family safe. To be honest with you, I don't know what agreement my father has already made with Tao Lee, and if they come for us, I need to make sure that you and Amirah are far away. My mother may agree to leave with you. I've sensed her distance from my father, and like you and Amirah, they are my family. Before we go though, we will be getting married, but the honeymoon will just last longer than expected for you and the girls, okay?" he kissed me and tears escaped my weak eyes.

I couldn't think or even speak. The way he was kissing me gave me a euphoric high, and all I wanted was him. His hands traveled over my body, and my hands had already found my target. Pulling his thick hard dick out, I moved down and took him into my mouth. His hand hit the desk as I slowly swallowed him and then let him slip right out my mouth. I knew my baby liked it sloppy as fuck, so I spit on his dick and then went to work. I sped up and felt him grab my hair. Sucking

2

harder around his base, he started to grip my hair and stroke back. This was the shit I loved. I would gag, and he kept going making my pussy jump. Sticking two fingers in my pussy, I played with my clit while still sucking the skin off Amir's dick.

He started to stiffen up, and I knew he was going to cum. Taking my free hand, I pinched my nipples and moaned, making him release right down my throat.

I stood up smiling and wiped my mouth, "Guess that office bathroom was a good idea, huh?" I giggled, walking over to the bathroom and grabbing some warm towelettes.

"I know you don't want to leave, and I know you have school to worry about, but O, I promise to make this work for us both. I just want to keep you and my family safe and out of harm's way," he said, looking through me.

"I know baby, and since this is what needs to be done I got you, but you should teach me the ropes, Amir. I know, I know. This ain't what you want your wife into, but what if something happens. I mean, Lord forbid, but we have to think like that," I said, taking this time to point out how the girls and I can help.

"O, that shit is dead man. Look we going to get married this weekend and y'all are leaving then as well. You might want to start your packing and shopping. Please don't fight with me on this one, okay. Just trust that your husband knows what he is doing, okay?" He kissed my forehead and walked out the office doors.

I stood there, arms crossed with a heated look. I don't get it. He didn't want to teach me fine. I would teach myself and still hold him down. After everything that we had been through, I couldn't believe he would leave me out of this.

When I entered the living room again, Isabelle and Israel were both sitting down with Amir and looking at me. From what I saw, they thought this was a great idea, and I didn't even plan to act like I did.

"So you guys are okay with just up and leaving? I mean Israel what about school and your friend?" I asked, sitting around with them.

"Octavia, this isn't about us or you. We want to keep the ones we love safe. We all played a part in this mess whether for the right or wrong reasons," she said, looking at Israel. "But we have to keep the innocent ones safe, and that's our families and friends," Isabelle said.

Thinking about what she said, I looked at Amirah who was giggling in her father's arms. She was innocent and it was her family who would hurt her. All this could be fixed if Amir would marry the disowned granddaughter, but this shit wasn't right. As much as I wanted to question him, I had to trust him and go with his lead. Amir has never let me down, and I have to let him lead, but he better believe I'm right behind him just in case.

"I guess we can make this a wedding and packing party," I said smiling. Something good has to come from this.

Chapter Thirty

EMERALD

Since I was still invited to the wedding, I decided to do some shopping. Everything with Trez and me was working out, and I wasn't hiding out anymore. I have spoken to both Bella and Octavia and apologized. Bella wasn't for it at first, but it took some time for her to come around. Tay was understanding, but even with everything going good, I still felt horrible for still lying in the first place.

Looking around Camille La Vie, I went with a short floral dress that was beaded lace and stitched closure in the back. I continued to look around to make sure I brought babe options to look at.

"I guess homewreckers shop here. Raya, let's go," I heard, so I turned around, and sure enough Santana and Soraya were standing there supporting smug looks.

"Tana, hello, it's nice to see you. Excuse me," I said, trying to walk past to the register. I had only found three dresses, but oh well. I wasn't about to mess with her while she had Simone with her.

"Oh, I know you're not trying to spend her nigga's money?" Soraya yelled and snatched the card from my hand. I turned to check her and felt a swift blow to the left side of my face. I couldn't see shit but red as I fell to the floor.

"Fuck Tana, some glass got stuck in Simone's head. Bitch, we have to go," I heard Soraya say, but I was drifting off.

I felt someone over me and could hear people screaming to call 911. "You might want to keep your distance," Tana whispered and rushed out the store, and everything went black.

❧

When I woke up, I could only see out my right eye, but my whole face hurt. It felt like I was the little drummer boy playing a marathon on my head. I tried to sit and felt a pair of hands come from my left side.

"Emerald, you're okay love. Do you know what happened to you?" Tay said with Bella right beside her.

"Where is Trez?" I asked, looking around for any sign of him being here.

"He went to check on Simone. Tana rushed her to the ER right before we got word you were here. He said he would be here when he found out about Simone. What happened, Emerald?"

"What did Santana say happened to Simone? Is she okay?" I asked, trying to get out the bed. I would worry about what happened to me later. Plus, I couldn't tell them that their best friend and her sister did all of this shit, Trez wouldn't believe me and neither would they.

BOOM!

The room door flew open and in charged Trez. "So you just run up on my baby momma with my daughter, bitch?" he said, wrapping his hands around my throat.

"Move, Trez! What the fuck kind of shit is you on, nigga?" Bella said, trying to pull him off me. He stepped back and looked as if he wanted to kill me.

"So, what happened then, huh Emily or Emerald?" he said sarcastically.

"Trez, I told you I was hitting the mall for a dress for the wedding this morning. I went alone as usual, and while I was shopping, they came in making jokes. I saw Simone sleeping in the stroller, so I went to check out, only for her sister to snatch YOUR card from me saying I'm spending her sister's money. When I went to get the card YOU gave me back, I was hit with something. Whatever she hit me with shattered and hit Simone that's when they rushed out." I said now amped up.

"Wait that's why they had to remove glass pieces from your scalp and hair," Tay said, looking at Trez.

I just stared at him with tears streaming. Just like I said, he didn't believe me.

"Yeah, that's what I just went through. Tay, I won't be making it to the wedding. Can I just have some privacy to rest?" I said and turned to face the wall. I had nothing else to say to Trez. I was really done.

Hearing the door close, I turned back over only to see Trez sitting across from me with his face in his hands. "Why are you still here? Simone needs you."

"Because Emerald, look I ain't mean what I said—"

"No you meant it Trez, and that's what hurts. I knew if I came and told you what really happened it was a good chance that you wouldn't take my word for it. I know I have lied in the past, but if we are going to have a future, you have to start giving me a chance."

"I know, and I'm sorry, okay? I just lost it seeing Simone like that, and when I spoke to Tana she gave me this story about you attacking her, and you threw a glass bottle. Look, it won't happen again."

"How is Simone?" I asked. I didn't want to argue or fight. My head was already banging enough.

"She had to get stitches, but she is okay. They're looking into it, but thanks for your side of the story, Em. I gotta go see what they plan to do," he said, getting up and coming to kiss me on my forehead before leaving out the room.

I blew a sigh of relief because I thought I had lost him, and I didn't want that. I heard my door open, and I sat back up. "That was quick ba—" I stopped mid-sentence with my mouth wide open.

"So you must have forgotten moms plan, huh? She takes you in, and this is how you repay my mother? Trez was to be delivered months ago. What is the holdup, Emerald?" Ava said, standing at my bedside.

"Ava, what are you doing here? He could have seen you and ruined everything. I have things under control. He will be front and center after the wedding," I said, rolling my eyes.

"I'm not dumb or blind, so don't try that 'I just need time shit' with me. Once you bring Trez, we can continue our plans. You have until Sunday morning when the sun touches your bedroom." She removed a piece of hair from my face with an evil grin and walked out the room.

I just pulled the covers over my head. Once I got out of here, I couldn't wait to leave and be far away from them— all of them.

Chapter Thirty-One

AMIR

After the big reveal from my father, I called a meeting to go ahead and get things together. Trez and Bleek already knew what the plan was, so I just needed to get the other men on board. I had a few young niggas who were hungry, and I planned to feed them all. My father thought that I couldn't handle it, but he was well mistaken. He had shown me well, and I needed him to let me be the man he raised.

Standing at the head of the table, I looked around at what I built. I wanted my empire to roam this land, and I was almost to the top.

"The Lee family wishes to step to us, and I think we ain't looking to be stepped on. I need niggas to tighten up around here. Y'all been on ya shit, so I ain't going to bust no ball, but stay alert. Them niggas move fast, and you will never see it coming," I said, looking at every soldier that I had in the room.

"They're aiming for families, and they won't stop until they have your heads. We advise you keep your family safe, but don't let our spots go. Keep them shits on lock," Trez added.

"Boss man, what about this shipment that we getting tomorrow?" Dre asked.

"We never switch up, so if they want it, come get it, but I want y'all to be ready to come and get it, iight?" I said.

"Man, so we risking our lives for you and yours to pick up and leave?" a kid named Malik asked with a smug look.

"Nigga, have you lost your mind?" Bleek started to go for him, but I stopped him.

"Nah, see that wasn't on my agenda, but when you see the person who gave you that bright idea, thank them." And I watch Dre send one to his dome.

That's what I meant by hungry. If niggas wanna step I let them, but if the wrong thing comes out, ain't no second chances. With a head nod, he sat back down, and Tubbs carried Malik's body out.

"Look, it's work to be done, and if you ain't built for it let me know now, and we can end business right now. Ain't no running, we fighting these niggas for our shit. We worked for it, so they ain't about to just take our shit. It's business as usual, but everybody stay on high alert. When we ready to move on 'em, I'll send you the code. Y'all are dismissed." I stood and watched them all leave.

"What now, Amir?" Bleek asked with Trez beside him.

"Y'all go spend some time with ya families before we have to go. I gotta got holla at my baby momma about this shit. I wanna see what all she knows," I said, dapping them both us and parting ways.

I knew Soraya to be nothing more than a snake. Each and every time some drama happened she is surrounding the cause. I know she knew something, and she wasn't going to keep putting my family through because I won't be with her. Pulling up to her house, I noticed Tana's car was there as well. I knocked on the door, and Soraya opened the door with hardly anything on.

"Man, put some clothes on and come back out to talk," I said, turning around. I ain't gone to lie my mans rocked up, and I didn't want to have any more mishaps.

"Amir, I am dressed, and you know you can come in. I mean you pay the bills round here anyway," she said, turning on her toes and going further into the house.

Walking inside, the house was a mess. Trash was overflowed, and it was pizza and Chinese takeout leftovers all over the place.

"You can't clean up, huh? And you wonder why Amirah isn't staying overnight with you. Look at this place, Raya. It's a fucking pigsty, and Amirah would put it all in her mouth. Do you get that?"

"Well, if you feel some type of way you clean that shit up, Amir. I ain't about to clean up shit if I don't have to. Matter of fact, how about you hire a maid to come clean all this shit up," she said, and I lost it.

I grabbed her by the neck and pushed her against the wall squeezing with all my might. "Soraya, I came to speak to you about yo actually keeping your child, and yet you still ain't ready. You got Tana all in me and my wife's face—"

"Nigga, fuck Octavia!" she yelled.

Dropping her ass I shook my head. She didn't want anything to do with Amirah. She just wanted the benefits of being her mother.

"You know what, you can have this shit, Raya. I might just lose my freedom messing with your dumb ass. You wanna see my daughter you come to my house," I said and left her, sitting there on the floor. I wanted to work with her, but I couldn't. She wasn't having the shit.

"Nigga, you will see me again. I don't need your ass!" she yelled at my back as I got inside my car. She thought her grandfather and his pull put fear in my heart. Nah, I was good. I didn't carry a label for a reason.

I was heading home and decided to stop by and finally speak to my father. What he did in my house, he could have come run by me first. I would never ambush O like that, and I know she was feeling salty. He needed to learn his place now. He was out of the game.

Walking into my parents' townhouse I saw no sign of my mother. I walked towards my father's office and heard talking. Leaning my ear against the door, I could hear him on the phone with someone.

"Don't worry she will be eliminated, and my son will control his temper. We will handle this so that it's is accidental," he spoke, and I couldn't believe my ears.

"As long as it is handled before the wedding day. My family will not show dishonor any further," I heard Tao Lee as well.

Moving back from the door, I rushed out the house. I hit the highway and headed for my wife. My father was doing just as I thought, and I wouldn't put it past him to already have someone on my house.

I pulled out my phone and tried to reach O but got her voicemail. I tried three more times and gave up. I called Trez and had him go by the house, and he said she wasn't home. I told him an address to meet up with me and told him to have Bleek and Dre there as well.

I didn't know where O was, but I knew she had better turn up sooner or later. My father always went through with his plans, and no mission goes undone that prevents mistakes. He was indeed a man of his limited words.

Just as I was pulling up to the meet spot, O called, and I had her meet us where we were. I needed my wife in on this one, and I knew that after the talk we had, she would be down. It was time to put them niggas away for good.

Chapter Thirty-Two

KIMBELLA

S hit had been crazy since war had been declared. We didn't go anywhere and stepping out was my life. I know we were in danger, so we all took turns turning up at each other's houses. Tubbs had even become one of the girls by now.

He was now taking me to my father's house where he moved in with Ms. Patrice. He was really loving her, and I loved to be around them. When I feel myself about to beat Bleek in the head, they always help me find my way.

"Hellooo!" I yelled when I walked into the house.

"We're back here, sweetie." I heard Ms. Patrice say from the back room.

"Hey, y'all. What are y'all doing back here?" I asked, walking into the back den.

"Girl, trying to find a movie to watch with your father, but he's being difficult. He knows I don't want to watch nothing with no whole lot of killing. He wants to see *Transporter,* and I just saw the trailer, so that's out," Patrice said.

"Now Patty, you know it's not even that bad. And I'm right here, so I'll hold you," he said, pulling her close to him.

"That's nasty. Ummm, I need to talk to you guys about something," I said, taking my seat across from them both.

"What's wrong, baby girl? You know we can make it through anything," my father said, sitting up and grabbing my hand. I smiled as Patrice sat up and touched his shoulder. Leaning in, it was as if their strength came into me.

"Bleek and I will be going away for a while, and I need to know that you will be okay. I mean if you guys want to come with us, I would love that idea," I said.

They both sat there looking at one another as if they were speaking with their eyes. I couldn't read their expressions, but I needed to know what I needed to do.

"Kimbella, can I speak with you alone up in the front?" Patrice asked and got up to leave. I looked at my father confused because he usually took the lead on things like this.

"Yes ma'am," I answered, getting up to follow her.

When I got to the living room, I watched her walk to her mini grandfather clock and pull a joint from behind it. "Ms. Patrice, does my daddy know you smoking weed?" I questioned in a hushed tone. I was smiling ear to ear, and she just giggled at me.

"Girl, he's got his habit, and I have mine. The difference is mine is healthy, and his was killing him. Come out on the patio," she said, and we went and sparked up. I don't know where she gets her weed from, but this was the shit I needed. "I know how them men get down that y'all are with, and I know you love him, so why are you questioning his moves?" she asked, catching me off guard.

"I'm not it's just I don't wanna leave daddy, he is all I have and—"

"No you have Bleek now, and your dad has me," she said, and I cocked my neck because we always had each other, neither of them could come between that. "What I am meaning is you two now have extra time for yourself. He isn't taking you from your father sweetie, he is just giving you both some space. All you can do it fill it when you can. Now go and have some fun. We will see you when you get back."

"We aren't leaving until after the wedding, so I have a day. That's why I came, we been on lock, so I had to see daddy before we left. Thank you, Patrice. I am so happy that we found you. This is the happiest I have ever seen my father, and that's all because of you," I said, speaking nothing but facts. My father had quit drinking and started attending church on a regular.

"Well, we both do our share, so the feeling is mutual. Just know you can have it too. Bleek seems to want to continue giving you this, early at that, so don't miss out. Leave my roach too. I know how y'all young folk get down," she said over her shoulder, and I just shook my head.

I spent a few more hours with them and then had Tubbs take me home. On the way to the house, we stopped to get Cook Out, and I could have sworn I saw Santana getting in the car with Tao Lee, and she was smiling like everything was all good.

Taking my phone out, I took pictures and made sure I sent them to Tay. This bitch was really falling off. After what happened in the hospital, Trez told her ass he wanted his daughter more and at his home with Emerald, or he was going to make sure they knew what really happened. She still has yet to take Simone by there. At least I knew why she had been so distant and standoffish with us. Now I couldn't wait for Tay's Bachelorette party.

Chapter Thirty-Three

SANTANA

I had just pulled up to my mother's new home, and I had to sit back in amazement. I guess my grandfather set her ass up too. My grandfather showed up out of nowhere, and at first, I didn't want shit to do with his ass.

One night when he showed up Soraya was with him all iced out and smiling ear to ear. He told me the story and how my mother chose my father over the family and ran away. I was so mad that I couldn't even pick up the phone for confirmation.

Ever since then he had been there for Simone and me where Trez had been lacking. The disrespect from everyone had been real, and not once had he ever checked his niggas or his bitch. The girls cut me off, and I didn't give a fuck. I had a best friend all this time, and I had been beefing with her.

Soraya had really stepped up in the twin department. She would watch Simone's whiny ass when I needed to make some extra cash, or meet up with Tao. I should have been took her advice and cut their asses off, but now they'll have to fall with them bum ass niggas they been with.

The only person I wanted safe was my father and his family. I understood they had their issues, but he was my father, and Maddison was my other little sister as well. I needed to make sure my mother and grandfather understood that. They were innocent in this matter if you asked me.

Getting out the car, I went around to grab a screaming Simone from the car.

"Shut up Simone, with your spoiled ass. I swear your daddy got you rotten and his dumb ass ain't helping deal with it," I fussed, walking up to my mother's door.

She kept fussing and screaming, so I popped her a few times.

"Ahhhhhhhhh, that's what that stupid shit gets you. I done told you," I said while she continued to wail out.

"Damn, shut that baby up. That's why Amirah don't come here cause I can't do that fucking fussing and shit," Mae said, opening the door and walking away.

"No, Amirah isn't here because Soraya doesn't even have her. I have my child, thank you. Where are we with this plan? I don't need any mess up," I said, knowing that she and Raya were good for them.

"Everything is set in stone like before. Nothing has changed. The best part is they won't even see it coming," she hissed, lighting a cigarette.

"Damn, can you put that out. I have to take her to Trez when I leave here, and I don't need him all in my face," I said, fanning the smoke.

"Bitch, neither you nor that child is special. Take her in the other room or leave; that's your choice." She continued to puff her Newport, and I gathered my shit and left. I was over the days of having to deal with her bullshit. I just needed her for this plan to go as Tao said. Knowing her, she would make a side deal in a minute because I knew how much she hated his existence.

Making sure Simone was dry and had everything she needed, I removed her from the car and went to knock on Trez's front door.

"Well hello, pretty," Emerald said from the other side when the door opened.

"Oh hell no bitch, you and Trez got me fucked up," I said turning on my heels to get back to my car. Suddenly, I felt Trez yank me back by my arm.

"Bitch, you got me fucked, not the other way around. She's staying and that's final you got a problem, take that shit up with your crazy self!" he barked, taking Simone out of my arms and she calmed down immediately.

"Trez, my daughter will not be staying here and nah you don't have no fucking final say so in shit. Yeah, I fucked up and beat that bitch ass while she was right there, but the bitch had it coming. Shit, for all I know so do you for walking out on us like you have. Now give me my damn daughter!" I screamed and reached for Simone and he moved, making me slip and scratch the bottom of her leg.

Simone screamed out so loud that I had to step back and look around. She continued to scream, and when I located the scratch, I saw it was deeper than I thought. Blood was dripping, and I started to panic. Trez looked like he wanted to kill me while still trying to calm Simone down. I couldn't move until I saw Emerald come from the house and grab Simone.

All I saw was red as I rushed Emerald, but Trez caught me by the hair and threw me to the ground. I had to grab my head because that fucker was banging. "Bitch, you're fucking crazy, and I should put one in your ass right now. Leave and do not ever come back, and maybe I'll let you live. I don't care who nut sack you descended from, that one is mine too, and you will never hurt her again," he whispered and got up, going after Emerald and Simone.

Getting myself together, I hopped in my car and sped off. Tears clouded my eyes, and I drove. All I wanted was for his ass to pay. Trez could have held me down and been there for me— they all should have. My grandfather may have given up on my mother, but he was giving me and Raya a chance to come up and now Trez, Bleek, and Amir had more that Tao Lee to worry about.

Chapter Thirty-Four

AVA

"Fuck, Bleek, right there don't stop!"

"Yeah, you like when I punish this pussy. That's why you keep showing you pretty ass, huh? You want daddy to spank that ass?"

"Ahhhh, shiiiit! Yessss, daddy!"

"Turn over and toot that ass up then, and don't play with me either!"

SMACK!

"Who pussy is it?"

"Ahhhhh, shiiiiiiit!"

SMACK! SMACK!

"That's not what I asked. I said who pussy is it?"

"Yours, Braylen! Fuck, it's yours!"

"Oooohhh shit!" I moaned as I came all over my twelve-inch dildo watching Bleek and Bella make love on my fifty-five-inch TV. I swear them smacking sounds, plus my surround sound make a bitch cum hard as fuck.

Putting my baby away, I turned the TV up while they went to the shower to finish. I love to role play like I was with them, so I decided I should shower and prepare for my day.

After my shower, I sat back and watched the footage to see what they were doing today. Suddenly, Brandon walked into the room, and my heart stopped. I watched him take baby steps over to a smiling Bella.

"Bitch, you need to be dressed. Damn, he's only a kid. He don't need to see that shit. You probably didn't even brush ya damn teeth!" I yelled at the screen.

I missed Brandon, and I wish I didn't have to do what I was doing to him, but he was part of the plan. I didn't know I would grow so attached to his chunky self, but I did, and it was killing me that to kill his father, I would have to put him in harm's way.

Bleek agreed to take them on a family date, so I jumped up and got dressed as well. It's a family date, so his mother should be there, right? I grabbed my keys and heard them say Dave and Busters, so I hopped in Toyota Camry and was on the way.

When I arrived, I parked in the handicap and waited to see them walk in. About twenty minutes later, I saw them walking hand in hand towards the entrance of Concord Mills. They had mommy, daddy, and son shirts on and the shit was low key cute. I kept my head down as they passed my car. When I thought they were gone, I sat back up just as Bleek looked my way. He squinted his eyes, and I smiled and waved. Bella's back was to me, and I started my car and pulled off. I saw him reach for his gun and I hit the gas.

I laughed thinking of how that nigga wanted to kill me in front of all those people and our son. He was just a pawn in my game though, and when I was done with him, I would dispose of him like I did the rest. Bleek thought he had everything on lock like Amir, except like Amir, he was a fool.

I knew so much about the operation and faces that I knew I could turn. I worked for them for seven years before I got pregnant with Brandon all the while holding my own agenda. He had so many chances to take me down, and yet he didn't. Bleek felt something for me and that's where he fucked up.

When he saw me with Janet, I was trying to get info on Trez. Luckily for me, they were tailing her like I thought, and they took me too. Things happen for a reason my mother always told me and this was true, but she also made sure I knew some things had to be done.

Back at my house, I turned my TV on the truck camera and waited for them to get back into the car. While I waited, I grabbed my phone scrolling for the number I needed and hit send.

"What? You need to text before you call me, okay?"

"Sorry Ma, but I have some news. We have a problem."

"What now?" she screamed.

"Amir has raged a war with the Lee family, and Trez is also in the middle of that war."

"Because of his dealings with Santana Lee, the granddaughter. This is not good news. I think they can handle this war, and we can take our place then. Come home," she said and hung up.

I sat there looking at my phone in disbelief. She promised Brandon would be coming with me when I came home, so I didn't understand. Tears threatened to fall from my eyes just as Bleek and Bella started to enter the car with Brandon.

I sat there and watched them both interact with my son and how his chunky face would light up when they called his name. He was so happy, and I had nothing to do with his every day joy. I watched helplessly and silently cried, wanting to scream that I was also just a pawn.

Feeling completely useless, I got up and began to pack my things. If I didn't return like I was told, she would come get me and that would ruin the plan and more would get hurt. I didn't want to risk Brandon's safety any more than I already had. No matter what I had done in the past, I was done hurting and using my son.

Once I was completely packed, I jumped in my car and hit the highway towards Athens, Georgia. I let the wind blow each tear away as I drove further and further from the one man I truly loved. Saying a quick prayer, I asked God to watch over my baby boy and to let him grow and learn that I love him too and that one day he would grow to forgive me.

Chapter Thirty-Five

SORAYA

Things had been looking up for ya girl lately. My grandfather had been taking care of me, and I didn't miss out on a damn thing. Amir thought he had the upper hand, but once we killed the weaklings, he would marry me and take care me of me like he should have been doing. Amirah was supposed to be my meal ticket, and he thought he was going to continue to raise her with Octavia.

I had already been in contact with Tao since I mysteriously found out he was my grandfather. The amount of muscle he carried with him could wipe Amir and his army off the face of this earth. Lucky for me we needed Amir to be the face of the brand we plan to create.

Running my hand through my hair, I sat on my balcony smoking some of the best weed to every grace these lungs. All the shit I had to go through just to get here was worth it. I told Tao everything I knew about Amir and his operation, and where all his spots were. Tomorrow at the wedding they were all getting hit and while they're getting hit Tana and I plan to set this wedding off— Lee style.

Getting up, I was startled by a knock at my front door. No one should be coming by, and I know my security didn't just let anybody up here. Taking my time, I walked into my room and put my sheer robe on and started towards the door.

"Who is it?" I yelled through the door.

"Man, open up Raya. I need to talk to you about some shit, man," Bleek answered from the other side.

Smiling, I opened the door and turned to walk away. I knew he was watching my ass through the sheer fabric, and I knew he wanted me—who didn't.

"What you need, Bleek?" I asked, turning around, except he wasn't behind me.

"Aye, sorry. I had got a call, and I took it outside. Look what's up with Trez and Tana? This new bitch has gotta go, Raya," he confessed and sat right across from me.

"What you mean? Your boy been dropped my sister, and her dumb ass let him. You don't like your new sister-in-law?" I joked in a mushy voice.

"Man, look. Between you and me she seems suspect like she's trying to do some shit. You think you could ask Tana to come around more or something?" Bleek said, getting up and walking over to me.

"Nigga, let me find out you need me. What is Bella going to do when she finds out I took another man of hers?" I asked, sliding down between his legs as he sat.

Pulling his huge dick out, I couldn't even contain how wet my mouth got. Taking him into my mouth, I swallowed him whole and licked his balls while his dick was completely in my mouth.

Click!

"Bella doesn't plan on letting you do shit. That's not why he is here," Bella said with a gun to the back of my head.

Bleek smiled and eased himself out my mouth, and if it weren't for this butt ugly bitch behind me with the gun, I would have bit his ass.

"Thanks for the head." He chuckled, zipping his pants and pulling his gun out too.

"So y'all came to kill me? Really? I would think someone more seasoned would do that, like my child's father," I said, smiling.

"Oh nah, we ain't want Amirah to have to hear that her father killed her mother so why not say Auntie and Unk did that shit cause it needed to be done, ey?" Bleek said, and I just rolled my eyes.

"Well, this won't turn out good for either one of you if you get my drift. Tao will find you, and when he does, you will all feel his wrath. Does Amir even know you are here?"

"Look I don't have time for the game because honestly, I don't give a fuck about this shit. I just want your snake ass dead. You have caused my family enough pain, and for what, to take seconds on dick every time around? At some point, you have to have some value for yourself, huh?" Bella said, making my blood boil.

"You know what, she's right. Babe, you're right. Raya, you will always on the next dick coming, and that's what got you fucked up," Bleek continued to joke.

"If you are going to shoot me pull that trigger bitch, but I don't need to hear all that yaya shit," I said. I didn't have time for the chastisement. I was ready to die if that's what was next for me. Either way, I knew they were about to get theirs, and I would see them both in hell.

I didn't hear it, but I felt the first bullet pierce through my shoulder, then a huge blow to the head. I fell to the ground, grabbing my throat trying to breathe as I watched them both run out the living room and out the house.

Visions of Santana and me playing at the park and of my mother and father being happy played in my head as I chocked on the blood rising in my throat. I tried to turn, but I couldn't move, I was beginning to get weak and going in and out of consciousness, I knew then that I wasn't making it and this is how my family would see me.

Just as my eyes got heavy and I could no longer hold them open, I heard my father's voice, and then Maddison's and Tamia. "It's okay, sissy. You can be with us now," was all I heard before everything went black.

Chapter Thirty-Six

AMIR

Looking at my phone I saw that the job was done, meaning after I handled this, things would be set for our wedding. I looked up just as Emerald was walking into the hotel room in a royal blue evening gown. Easing out of my car, I followed her to the elevators. There were two henchmen in the elevator when it opened, so I ducked behind a plant making sure she was still visible.

"I don't know if she can handle this, Amir. I mean she is just as innocent as I was when we first got together. The only reason you're using me now is because I showed my loyalty and strength. What are we going to do?" O asked, walking up behind me hiding as well.

I didn't even reply. I had seen Emerald handle her fair share of niggas, so I wasn't worried at all. Seconds later the elevator doors opened again, and I pulled O from hiding. We walked into the elevator, and Emerald was standing there, and the guards were gone.

"Oh well, excuse me sir, and you look radiant, ma'am," she said, walking out of the elevator.

"Thank you. Why don't you join us?" O said, and I just shook my head as the elevator doors closed.

"Iight, y'all stick to the plan okay. No bullshit and Improvising," I said as the elevator doors opened.

We walked into my father's suite and eased around the corner as we heard laughing coming from the office. We eased back, and I shook my head at the girls. I told them to fall back because it was just them two. O hesitated and then followed Emerald to be ourlookouts.

I kicked the door in, and sure enough, my father was standing in front of Tao Lee holding a glass of Whiskey. Putting my gun dead center on Tao, I smiled and got closer to them both. "Well, I guess the plans have changed, father. You cross me for a bigger bank account? I'm your fucking son, and I would never do that to your wicked ass." I was hurt like a muthafucka.

"Put that shit away before you regret ever walking into this suite!" Tao yelled, jumping up only to catch one straight between the eyes. He fell to the ground, and my father pulled from behind his back and pulled out a gun. Before I could lift my shit up on his ass, I heard a gun go off and saw him drop as well over his desk. Whiskey stained the white fur rug when I turned around see Octavia coming from the back with her gun still on my father.

"O, what you doing still here man?" I yelled, scooping her into a hug. That shit was a turn on, but she could have hurt her damn self.

"I didn't feel right leaving you in here alone. We gotta go, Amir. They will be coming for him soon," she said, pulling away, and I followed her with my gun up just in case.

When we finally got home, we couldn't keep out hands off each other. For a man that had just killed his father, I felt nothing but the love and affection for my soon to be wife. We ran upstairs to get into the shower, O turned it on just how I liked it, and I helped her wash her body while teasing her nipples.

I continued until she started to beg me for more. "Amirrrr, fuck me! Fuck me before you make me your wife," she moaned aloud.

I rammed my dick just like she asked, and she bent all the way over. The water was beating on my back, and the juices were sliding down her legs. I was fucking her guts up.

"Just like that, Amir. Don't you fucking stop! Shit!" she screamed.

I pulled out and picked her up, I placed him inside her and began to bounce her on my dick. At first, she wanted to get down, but when I hit that spot, she tilted her head back and enjoyed the ride of her life.

"I'm about to cum, Amir. Cum with me. Give me a baby, Amir," she moaned, and I couldn't hold it back any longer.

I came long and hard inside O, and I prayed that she meant what the fuck she had just said cause I was sure Amir the second was in there. We went a few more rounds before the water started to get cold.

Laying with O in my arms felt so right, I had been with plenty of women, but there was something about O that made me want to switch my whole life up. She made me want to go legit and get things on track so that she doesn't have to continue to sacrifice so much.

"O, you still up bae?" I asked, rubbing her natural fro.

"Yes Amir, I can feel you staring at me, so I can't fall asleep. You okay?" she asked, sitting up looking at me.

"Yeah. I just want you to know how happy I am to finally make you Mrs. Amir Montee," I said, kissing her forehead.

"Awwww you can be such a sweetheart sometimes. I am happy you chose me though. I mean I know you had a few choices."

"Yeah, you right. A bunch of big booty bitches at my beck and call," I joked.

She punched me playfully in the arm but with much force. "Nigga, don't play. You see how I work," she said, laughing.

"Nah, you will never step to me like them other niggas, and look at you feeling yourself." I chuckled.

I was happy she was back to herself but worried because she enjoyed this shit. I could see it all over her face. O enjoyed killing Omari and had all reasons to. When it came to my father, it was just enjoyment.

Chapter Thirty-Seven

OCTAVIA

"Octavia Mills, you are going to ruin your make up with all that crying. Relax, this is the most amazing wedding, and it's all for you," my mother said, trying to calm me down, but I was going crazy.

Amir and the guys were late, and I know for a fact that he left the house when we did. I picked up my phone and tried dialing him again and nothing. I tried Trez and then Bleek who actually picked up.

"Hello?"

"Hello, my ass. Nigga, where the fuck is Amir, and he better be in this fucking church or—"

"Tay, chill. You're in the damn church. We are almost there. Something came up on the way here. We almost there though. Here nigga cause she ain't going to kill my ass today," he said, passing Amir the phone. I had to take a deep breath because he knew not to play with me on this day of all days.

"Babe, what the fuck? Where are y'all and what happened?" I ran off with questions and was now pacing.

"She's going to mess her hair up too, watch," I heard Bella whisper to Emerald and my mother, and I rolled my eyes.

"We're almost there beautiful, don't pout. Yeah, I know you over there showing your ass."

"Amir, you got one hour, and I'll be walking down the aisle. Fuck with me if you want to," I hissed and hung up, sitting back in the makeup chair.

"Is everything okay?" Bella asked, coming back to touch up my makeup.

"They will be because he about to be here and things going to work out right, Ma?" I asked, turning to her.

"Octavia, you're nervous, and that's perfectly normal. We all go through that. When I was preparing to marry your father, I almost ran from the church because his tie wasn't at the church. I ended up marrying him with no tie and more joy and happiness than I have ever felt. That man loves you, and he won't mess this up for you. Let us finish getting you ready for your big day." She smiled, and I felt better.

I let the ladies get me right while I sipped my wine and relaxed. We had handled everything we needed to make sure today was perfect for us. There was no reason for me to be stressing, Amir did love me, and he would be here no matter what.

I looked up and saw Emerald standing by the window in a daze. Getting up, I walked up to her to make sure she was okay. "Hey Em, you good?" I asked, noticing tears coming from her eyes.

"No, I mean yeah I'm fine. I just, it's all this wedding stuff. I don't know if it that's in the stars for Trez and me. I really don't think Tana will let us be happy not the way we want to," she started and wiped her tears. "I'm sorry. This is your day, Tay! No negative thoughts this way, right?" she finished, smiling and perking up.

"Em, he loves you, okay. Just like me, you can't question that. Just continue to be honest and upfront with him and also let him handle Tana. I don't know what happened to my girl, but she ain't the girl I grew with," I said, thinking back to our childhood days.

"That bitch found her roots that's what. Did you know they found Mike, Tamia, and Maddison in the Yadkin River this morning, Tay?" Bella said with tears running down her face, and her phone in her hand.

Grabbing her phone out her hand, I looked, and sure enough, it was them. Tears started to form, and I couldn't stop them from pouring from my eyes. I wanted to reach out to Santana, but I didn't even have her number anymore. Then I thought about it, why were Amir and the guys late? I prayed he didn't do this to get at Santana for trying him, but if he did there was no way I could marry him. "This couldn't be the reason—"

"No, Tay. Don't say no shit like that. Bleek and Amir wouldn't do that to Maddison." Bella cut me off, sounding like she was reassuring herself more than she was reassuring me.

"Why would they have anything to do with something so horrible?" my mother asked, looking at Bella and me.

"Why don't we give them some privacy and go make sure the guys have arrived," Patrice said, guiding my mother out of the dressing room.

"Bella, I need to get to Amir right now. This shit can't be happening right now," I said, fanning myself.

"Tay, pull yourself together and put on your damn game face. You will be getting married today, and it will be a beautiful ceremony. As soon as that ass touches the seat of that car, you wear into his ass about why the fuck he was late, and what the fuck he got going on without you. Then we can both go find Tana and be there for her, okay?" Bella said with her game face reigning strong.

"You're right, best friend. Let's get this bitch hitched!" I yelled wiping my face and putting my game face on.

Back to it again Bella began to beat my face for the Gods. Emerald pinned up my hair because I was not about to sit and wait for it to be curled again. I went to put my dress on and on the way out I passed a mirror and had to do a double take.

There I was, Octavia Mills once battered, bruised, and feeling less than what I really was. I was about to walk out this room and into the arms of the reason. Amir was my smile, my laugh, and even my cries. Tracing the dress with my hands, I was infatuated with how healthy I looked as well. Today would be perfect, and I hoped Amir knew when we left I wanted all my answers or it was no pussy, even on his wedding night.

Chapter Thirty-Eight

AMIR

Here I stand waiting for my heart to walk down the aisle. I ain't going to lie. I was nervous and scared. I was smooth with her, and I was calm. I could express myself with her and not feel defeated or less of a man.

My attention went to the doors as Simone and Amirah threw out their flower petals on the church aisle. Their assistant Israel was trying to keep them from eating the pedals, making everyone giggle, and me smile. My baby girl was growing up day by day, and she was so beautiful. Even with having my looks and name, she still carried a part of her mother.

Next, Brandon, accompanied by Bella and Emerald, walked down with the rings. He was a true playa and to be honest if O had it her way, he would be in the $30,000 tux, not me. I looked down at my mother, and the way she looked at me made my whole facial expression change. She knew, and she knew it had to be done, but she was hurting that she couldn't confirm it was me.

"Here Comes the Bride" began to play and the double doors opened. Looking up, I saw my future wife appear. She was beautiful and confident as she walked to me with her father on her arm.

"This is it, my nigga, don't mess this up," I heard Bleek whisper and laugh.

"Nah, I got her," I said just as she got to the altar.

I could see that she had been crying, but she still had a huge smile on her face when she looked at me. I loved the way her eyes always fill with light when I walked into the room or just looked at her. Her father passed her on to me with a stern look and a head nod, and the wedding began.

It's was time for me to say my vows and to be honest I didn't write shit, I was going to speak from my heart and keep it real.

"Octavia, when I met you, I saw the women you are today. Not the pain and the hurt from the past, but I saw who you were destined to be. What I didn't see was how you would change my life for the greater good. Before I met you, I was in shambles, fixing everyone else's problems and leaving mine to drown in my brain, so I didn't know it mattered. You showed me how to take care of myself and still leave room for everyone else, and that's why I made it clear we would be here today. Octavia, you own my soul now until the Lord calls me home, to keep it safe like you always have from the demons always after us. I love you Octavia Mills, and today you have made me the greatest, blessed man on earth," I said and meant every word.

"Amir, things for us have been a test, something that we always suppress. When I met you I was beaten and battered," she said, and I had to look around because I knew she said she didn't want that out there, so I made sure not to say anything.

"It's okay, I was, and I am not proud of being in that moment, but I am so proud of myself for growing with you. I never would have, and something about you made me take that leap. You keep me on my goals and push me to go harder. When things get tough for me, I know I can always call you or text you, and you will make things ten times better. Amir, we make each other great, and I can't thank God enough for blessing us with such a wonderful man. I love you, Amir Montee, forever and always," she finished, and Bella gave her a tissue to dab at her eyes.

I just smiled, I was the luckiest man on earth, and to be honest, I couldn't wait to take my wife away and celebrate.

We exchanged rings and finally heard what we had been longing for. "I now pronounce you husband and wife. You may kiss your bride, Mr. Montee."

"With pleasure." I smiled and kissed O Long and hard, while the audience cheered and clapped.

"You're so goofy," O whispered once I gave her some air. I couldn't help myself if we weren't in this church right now, I'd have my wife bent over somewhere calling the almighty right now.

"Are staying for the reception, or can daddy sneak you away for a minute?" I asked walking down the aisle with my wife. Everyone was smiling, even my mother who I was worried about.

"No. We are staying, Amir. Let's celebrate with everyone else now, and I got big daddy later," she purred in my ear, and I have to cover myself up cause my mans certainly rocked up hearing that.

We finally got down with the celebrating, and everybody was having a great time. I saw Bleek and Simone dancing, and her little chunky self was cheesing all day. She loved her some Uncle Bleek and didn't like Bella's ass. Nobody understood it, but Bleek was her homie. She just put up with us. My mother standing alone watching Israel and Tay dance around caught my eye. Pulling her aside, I wanted to know what was wrong.

"Mother, are you okay?"

"You have done what you had to do. It hurts to let go, but it was for the best. I am happy for you, Amir. Treat her like a queen and always include her, even during business. I love you son and make sure Octavia knows we love her too."

"Thank you, mother," I said, and she walked away. She knew what had happened and knew that it had to be done, but it didn't mean that it didn't still hurt knowing he was gone. I watched her walk away and went to find Trez and Bleek.

"I should have known y'all would be occupying the bar." I laughed, walking up on them.

"Man, Simone tired a nigga out brah, but congrats nigga you off the market now," Bleek said, taking a sip of his beer.

"Don't come for my baby, Bleek. You're just mad she dances

better!" we heard Emerald say, twirling Simone making her giggle and scream with glee.

"Tell him again baby!" Trez said smiling ear to ear watching them. I was happy for my niggas, and I knew it was only a matter of time before they were in the same shoes as me today.

"Trez, you caught up with Santana yet?" I asked, getting down to business.

"Nah, she's still ghost on a nigga, but she came by the house this morning, I do know that. Something ain't right, and I feel it. I think she's going to try something but not here," he said, putting his head down.

"I know, man. I don't know why Mike and his family went down like that, but Tana's gotta know we ain't have anything to do with that shit. I would never do that shit to Bella or Tay. Hell, Maddison was my homie," Bleek said, shaking his head.

I sat back and thought about it and couldn't really understand why they had to hurt Maddison and Tamia. Mike had his ways back in the day, but even he had gotten on a straight path and lived right by them.

"Well you know Dre never did find Mae. I think her and Tao did that shit to make Tana think it was us," Trez said I could tell he was holding back tears because he promised to take care of Mike and his family even after all this went down, especially Maddison.

"Can we handle this after my reception?" we heard from behind us, and O was standing in a short, cream laced dress and some cream red bottoms that made me want to take a hike up her legs.

"This isn't the place for this anyways. Come on, babe," she said, pulling me from the guys, and I damn sure went willingly.

She put her arms around my neck and danced to "The Way" by Arianna Grande. This was O's shit, and no matter how many times I tell her I don't like that pop music shit, she still made it appear on the song list. She swayed her hips and sung along with the song in my ear.

"Let this be the last time you try and check me in front of my friends," I playfully whispered in her ear.

"Oh no, I do what I want now. I'm Mrs. Amir Montee, and my name ring volumes round here," she said, sounding like me.

"You tried, but with that comes a lot— children, a bigger house, and more cars. More work as well," I said, looking into her eyes.

"What do you mean by that?" she said, looking a bit confused.

"I thought you said no business talk here?" I said, smiling cause I knew I had her attention.

Grabbing my hand, she pulled my ass all the way to the reception hall office. Pushing me in, she closed the door behind her and placed her hand on her hips and pouted like usual. "Now what did you mean by that?"

"Not here either, O. You don't run shit, and I ain't gotta say shit." I smirked.

"Oh really?" she asked, walking up to me and grabbing my hand and placing it between her legs.

"O, where the fuck is ya underwear at?" I said, tickling her already moist pussy. She moaned lightly as I used my thumb to massage her clit and stroked her in and out with two fingers.

"Now is not the time to judge, just give me a sample, and we can call it... uuuuuhhhh even," she said now gyrating on my hands. I couldn't hold my smile back as she tilted her head back and closed her eyes.

I pulled my hand out from between her legs and stood up. Pulling my slacks down I released the monster begging to come out, and her eyes lit up like a Christmas tree. She turned around and got on the desk tooting her ass all the way up in the air. I slid in and almost bust with the first stroke, her pussy was drenched and tight as fuck.

"Fuck O, your shit feels even better now that you mine for good. Throw that shit back for daddy," I groaned like a lil nigga, but the shit felt that good.

Doing as she was told, O threw that shit back, and I caught it every time. We were going so hard, and she was so loud that I knew we were going to get fucked up when we walked back in with everyone else.

"Ooooooohhhhhh right there, daddy! That's my ahhhhhhhhhhh!" O said and came all over my dick, and seconds later I followed.

I slowed down, but I wasn't done. I needed more of that good shit, and she knew I was down for all night in this room if I had to.

"No, Amir. We have to get back, and I know my damn daddy heard my ass," she whispered and hopped off the desk leaving my mans standing at attention.

"Nahhhh O, you can't do ya husband like that man. You worried about your daddy, but he puts ya moms to sleep too. How you think you got here?" I asked, fixing myself back up.

When she didn't respond I looked up, and her back was to me, but she was still facing the desk. I walked over to see what she was looking at and it was a picture of her Bella, and Tana with Maddison at about one sitting on O's lap.

"Why did things work out like this, Amir? I mean they were supposed to be here for me. Tana has been there since day one, and now she's switched up on me. Now her family is all gone, and I hate to say it, but when she comes for us, I want to be the one to put her down," she said with her back against my chest and her head leaning back on me.

"O, remember when your parents were talking divorce, and I told you sometimes we have to get that space to see if the heart grows fonder or further? Tana needed that shit, and unfortunately, she got mixed up in Raya and Mae's shit with Tao. I don't know for sure, but I think they did that to them."

"Is that why you were late to your own wedding? Looking for Mae?" she asked, turning to look me in my eyes.

"Nah, that's not why, but we can talk about that a little later," I said, pulling away and getting ready to walk out the door.

Looking back, I could tell that she was upset that I didn't give her what she wanted, but O had to let things happen.

"Fine," was all she said, and she walked out the room.

Joining everyone else, I watched her go straight to Em and Bella talking shit. I didn't care cause I'm sure they saw that walk when she came up, so they know she was just being petty. I went a joined the men until it was time for my big surprise. I wanted to do something for O that showed her that we were in this together and that this was OUR family, and we would take care of them no matter what.

Chapter Thirty-Nine

OCTAVIA

"And where did you and Amir drift off to, Mrs. Montee?" Emerald said, fanning herself and Simone while still bouncing to the music.

"Well, my husband had some business to discuss, and I didn't want to keep him waiting. He is a very powerful man you know," I joked, and they both burst out laughing. "No, but for real, he thinks Mae and Tao took out Mike and his family behind Tana's back to frame them, us. I don't know if she is thinking clearly, but we need to reach out to Tana and see where her head is at," I said, looking to Bella.

"Man, no I can't Tay. I love you, but I be damned if I come to her. She was our girl, and she snaked us out like that! Look at my niece's head, Tay. There is some shit you can't forgive, and I think Tana just has what's coming to her ass," she retorted and picked at her plate.

"She's right, Tay. You going over there or even calling her would be a sign of weakness, and she might use that to her advantage," Emerald said. "Let's see if she makes a move on you first, and when she does, we will all come for that ass, not you alone."

"I got me trust that, so I don't need any bodyguards," I said, feeling a tad bit offended.

"Oh, I know thugga thugga, but what I'm saying is when your

husband finds out don't you think he will be less pissed off if we were there with you?" she said, and the shit made sense.

"Iight, I just hope she is okay. As mad as I am with her, I know they didn't deserve that," I started and the tears wouldn't let me finish.

"Tay, come on. Let's get some liquor in you," Bella said, rubbing my shoulder and taking me to the bar with the guys. Emerald took Simone to James and Patrice, who had already knocked Amirah and Brandon out, and came to join us a few minutes later.

"Thank y'all for making this the most perfect wedding ever. I can say Bleek and Trez that y'all have become the best big brothers a girl could ask for. Bleek, you carry this flame for Bella, and since day one you have had my girl smiling. You have fucked up, but you made things right, and that's what men do," I said, starting to feel the drink.

"Man, Tay, take your drunk and sensitive self on nah. You know I got Bella; that's my heart. I plan to make her my wife one day real soon. After that she gonna be pregnant as fuck cause I need my football team," he said, slapping Bella on the ass. She mushed him in the face playfully and shook her head.

"If that's what he wants then he better start making the team now cause I need some time to live, but I got you, daddy," Bella said, winking and kissing Bleek.

I looked over, and Emerald looked away quickly. I knew she was feeling like this wouldn't be her, so I made sure she knew it would.

"Trez, you brought Emerald into my life, and I am grateful. She has shown a side I never knew she had, and now I question why you ain't beat Tana ass all them times?" I asked now really wondering.

"That was Trez's baby momma, so now when he gives me the go ahead, I'll be on her ass, but I ain't the get myself locked up for killing a bitch type of female. I handle mines, but she's got one coming for her," she said, eying Trez as if he would protest.

"Yeah man, what she said. I mean Tana was my heart, and I tried to fix her, but that shit wasn't working. I got tired of seeing my daughter in danger, man. That shit does something to you. Even after I left not knowing what could happen, and if you're going to get that call. Em's been down for me with all that shit and more," he said turning to Emerald, and I smiled instantly.

Getting down on one knee, Trez pulled out a ring box and grabbed Emerald's hand. "You know when I first found out your real name I wondered why? I figured hell maybe because she was green to everything I was all about, but you weren't. You hold me down and what you said was straight facts. I got you if you got me. Emerald Daye, will you honor me in becoming Mrs. Quantrez Jones?"

She covered her faces and tears just started pouring from her eyes. We smiled and waited for her response that never came.

"Em?" I said, rubbing her shoulder. "Answer the man."

"Yes, oh sorry! Yes, Trez, I will marry you!" she cried and bent down to kiss him.

"Told ya!" I screamed, sticking my tongue out.

A few weeks ago Trez had asked me how I felt about Emerald with everything that had happened, and I told him the truth. She was cool and sweet and seemed to love him and Simone. I knew this was coming, and she was worried for nothing.

Looking up at Amir, I noticed that I was too. Things have been so good for us since I gave him my trust and things could only go up for us. This had truly been the happiest day of my life. I looked around the room and smiled. "What more could a girl ask for?" I said to no one in particular.

"You do have it all," Amir whispered into my ear.

Smiling even harder, I turned around to face him. "So where are we going from here, husband?"

"Where would you go if you could go anywhere in the world?" he asked for the millionth time.

I sat back and really thought about where I really wanted to go, I had always wanted to visit Greece and sail the waters and even swim if I could. I wanted to travel and taste different foods and see their cultures.

"Greece," I said finally.

"Greece, it is then. Go tell the girls," he said, and I jumped for joy.

"Y'all, we're going to Greece!" I yelled, grabbing everyone's attention.

"Oh my gosh baby girl, when?" my dad said, smiling with my mother on his arm.

"Can I go with y'all? That's all I need to know," my mom joked, laughing.

They had come so far since their getaway last Christmas. I was so happy that they decided to work through things and make their marriage work. That was the main reason I knew I could pull this marriage off.

"We leave after this is all over actually. I just called and booked the flight." Amir said, grabbing me from behind and kissing my cheek.

"That's amazing. We can watch the kids so you all can have a break. I think that's fair." Patrice said, looking at my parents, and I looked over at Amir.

"That would be great. How about you guys watch them at your own Florida getaway?" he said, and their eyes all lit up like kids on Christmas morning.

"Oh no, Amir. You don't have to do that, my man. We would be just fine keeping them here in town," my father said, trying not to be a burden as usual.

"No, sir. I think we all could use the break from everything going on," Amir said, and my father nodded.

"I can't believe you. You're just full of surprises, huh?" I said, fixing Amir's tie.

"I mean I do what I can to put a smile on this one woman's face. But that ain't a big deal, that's my job."

"Well, you do that well, sir." I winked at him.

"Well actually I'm not quite finished yet," he said with a sly grin.

"What does that mean?"

"Damn Tay, can he ever just surprise you and you not question him?" Bella joked.

"To be honest, I want to know too because nothing can top this," Emerald said with Trez's arms wrapped around her.

"Amir?" I asked just as his mother and sister walked back into the ballroom with some guy around Israel's age.

"Amir, I have someone I want you to meet," Israel said, grabbing his arm. "I just need him for one second, Octavia," she pleaded, and I followed my husband.

"Who is this, Israel?" Amir said in a stern voice, I sat back and watched as he sized the young man up and the poor boy didn't know what to do at this point.

"This is Ricky, my boyfriend that I was talking about. He got accepted to Howard, and I thought he could celebrate with us since his family didn't make time for him."

Looking at Ricky, he reminded me of someone, but I couldn't really figure out who. He was tall, but muscular, and had my milk chocolate skin complexion. He looked like he wanted to speak up, but wasn't sure what he would even say to my husband.

"Hello, I'm Octavia, his wife. We would love for you guys to join us, but it's slowing down. How about you two come vacay with us?" I asked, looking up at Amir to calm him down.

"Yeah, I can get to know you a little better," Amir said, keeping his focus on Ricky.

"Aww, thanks, brother. You are the best! Come on babe, let's go get packed," Israel said, pulling Ricky by the arm.

"Nice to meet you!" he finally found his voice.

"You didn't have to grill him like that, Amir," Isabelle said.

"He fucking her, so he better be ready for me if he fucks with her in any way," he said.

"Well, just run him off and let her be mad at you for the rest of her life? Wish Octavia had a big brother to push your big ass around Amir, you were wrong and you know it," she scoffed and walked out behind Israel.

Shaking my head, I helped everyone get what they needed and made sure the cleaners knew where to take my gifts, and I went to change so that we could head to Greece. It's was about to be lit.

Chapter Forty

AMIR

After finally dancing her heart out, O was ready to go. I had one more trick up my sleeves, and I wanted to capture her face when she saw her surprise. I made sure Trez and Bleek hadn't said anything to the other girls, especially Bella's ass cause she couldn't hold water for shit.

"O, come on. I got something else for you," I said, pulling her towards the entrance.

"Oh Lord, what more could you give me, Amir? Things were perfect as is," she said, walking out the door and to the street.

"Why we have to come if Tay is the one who has the surprise, and why didn't I know, Bleek?" Bella said, rolling her eyes.

"Because Amir knew how your mouth gets when your back is against the wall with Tay. You would tell her everything if you knew it would calm her down. Don't be mad, bae," Bleek said and winked at her.

"Here they go y'all," Trez said, rubbing his hands together and the look O had was priceless.

First to pull up was Octavia's black Benz with gold chrome. Followed by Belle's pink Bentley with black rims. Her tags read *Beep*

Beep cause Bleek said she had road rage like a bitch. Finally, Trez had gotten Emerald an all-black Tahoe with tinted windows.

"What in the entire fuck, bae? You ain't shit. I didn't even know you were looking at buying me a new car!" O screamed.

"Trez, you done fucked up here," Em said, passing him Simone and running to jump her short ass in her new truck.

"Bella, what you think?" Bleek said to Kimbella who was just staring at her car. Before she could reply, gunshots rang out of nowhere.

Pulling our guns out, we returned gunfire. I couldn't see what direction the bullets were coming from , but when I looked up James had gotten everyone in the building, and Trez was running towards the Tahoe. O and Bella were both bussing at an all-black BMW that was also shooting towards them.

"O, get the fuck down out here! NOW!" I barked. I ran to get to her and saw Bella fall back.

Bleek shot the nigga who caught Bella and ran to her aid. O kept bussin' at one car in particular, and when I looked up, it was Santana Lee aiming right for her. I ran and threw her to the ground just as the bullet flew by her head missing by inches. We all got down and finally heard tires screeching.

I stood up, and the cars we had just purchased were fucked, but that didn't mean shit to me. Bella was laid out and had caught one in the arm. Bleek pulled out his phone and called Tony, our personal doctor, to meet him at his house to get Bella straight. Looking over O, I saw she was good, but she was more worried about Bella and Emerald.

"Aye man somebody come help me, man!" Trez yelled from the Tahoe.

O shot up and ran to the car and let out a gut-wrenching scream. Emerald laid there with a shot to the leg and one to the chest. She was breathing , but it was short and labored.

"What we going to do, Amir? we need to get her to the hospital," O said, trying to keep an eye out on Bella and Em.

"I got it. Get her in the back. Bleek, take Bella and make sure she's good and y'all meet up with us at the hospital." I helped Trez carry Em to the back where O sat and laid her on her lap.

"Stay with us, Emerald. We're going gotta find that bitch together, you hear me?" O said as Trez hopped in the passenger, and we pulled off.

"She good, Tay?" Trez yelled.

"I don't know, Trez. She's closing her eyes and shit, so y'all need to hurry the fuck up."

"Just try and keep her up, babe. We're almost there," I said, looking at her blood-stained dress through the rear-view mirror.

I couldn't believe Santana was that bold that she attacked us all at my fucking wedding. This just confirmed what I had been thinking all along. She thought we killed her father and sister. I didn't know where O's head was at, but I prayed she didn't run off and to get at Tana alone.

The power she displayed today was mostly a warning that she was coming. When she came back for us, it would be harder, and she better believe we were going to be ready.

Turning into the hospital ER unit, I went to put the car in park and Trez had already jumped out to get Emerald out. O and I followed them inside and waited to hear from Bleek and Bella.

"What happened?" the doctors asked, wheeling her to surgery.

"We were leaving a wedding, and there was a drive-by with some local thugs. She was getting in the car, and the car was in the way," O said, looking at Trez and me.

"Man, just save her fucking life! Fuck the rest save my girl, man," he said, shaking his head.

They nodded and rolled her into surgery. Trez watched until he couldn't see her anymore and then turned the punch the wall. "Man, this some bullshit! Who the fuck could have done some shit like this?"

"It was Santana," O said, walking up to him and laid her hand on his shoulder. He yanked away and got into her face, and O didn't even flinch.

Jumping up, I got in between them cause Trez was tripping even thinking about that shit. "Nah not that one. She ain't did shit."

"Man, my bad Tay. You know this shit got me fucked up. How you know it was Tana, man?" he said sitting down.

"When the shit first popped off, I saw Bella looking dead at her. She wasn't hiding, and she wasn't scared. Hell, the bitch wasn't even in the cars until they sped off and that's how she got one in Bella," O said, pacing the floor. "She was aiming for Emerald, Trez. She knew she had to end her if nothing else today, and I pray she takes her time running because when I catch her, it's lights out."

"Damn, Bella was hit too?" Trez asked. "Yeah, Tana done lost it. Once Emerald is cleared to leave, we will be on that ass."

I sat there in disbelief of what was going on. Like why would Santana shoot up the place knowing her child and others were there. If she was really mourning her sister's death, why possibly cause more children's deaths. I struggled with trying to let everyone else have their say, but I was already on top of things. I wanted Santana in my face before we boarded this plane— dead or alive.

I called Bleek to make sure Bella was iight, and he said she was good. The bullet went straight through and didn't do too much damage, but it hurt like a bitch. I called Octavia's parents, and they said they would keep Amirah and Simone and that James and Patrice had already taken Brandon home with them.

I made sure Tubbs and Dre were also keeping their eyes on the hospitals and our homes. I didn't need Tana going after our families while I was away. I made a few more calls, and then the doctors came out, and we all went to see what happened.

"Ms. Daye and baby are fine. Surgery went well, but we want to keep her overnight just to make sure she is okay. Now she needs to rest, but you can go back in a few."

"Wait Doc, what you mean baby? Emerald didn't tell me anything about a baby," Trez said.

"Well she is about twelve weeks along, but the baby is strong and doing good," the doctor said and went back to check on Emerald.

"Well congrats, Trez. It looks like you're getting a wife and a baby all in one. Plus, my girl is going to be okay, so that's the biggest blessing of them all," O said, hugging him.

"Thanks, Tay. Man, I gotta another one coming and Simone ain't going to have that shit. I am glad Emerald is okay, man. That shit scared the fuck out of me man. I don't know what I would have done if anything had happened to her. Then to find out she is carrying my child, man that shit crazy," Trez said. "I wonder why she ain't say shit though before now."

"Man, don't dwell on that shit. She's good and breathing. That's all you need to be worrying about. O's parents have the girls, so you can stay up here. They're good. You need to get yourself together to go in that room and reassure Emerald that you got her and everything is going to be okay. Shit, the way Emerald be with Simone, you don't have shit to worry about man. Just keep her happy like you been doing. Show her how dedicated you are to her, man," I said.

"Man, I do that every day, and she knows that. I just wonder why she didn't feel comfortable enough to come and talk to me about it. She talks to me about everything, even that job she did with you and Tay that you thought I didn't know about." He looked up at me and O shaking his head and chuckling. "We keep our shit one thousand, so why wouldn't she let me be a part of this with her?"

"Maybe she really wanted to, but with everything going on, she figured it would be best after we all completed what we had going on. Tana was a lot on her and to find out that's she was going to keep coming for you like this. Give her a chance because if you go in there making her feel like she kept this from you for no reason, you would have just given her one. Emerald has made her mistakes, yes, but you have to be willing to see the growth for what is and not continue to push her back down to the old her," O said, sitting beside Trez.

He sat back and thought about what she had just said and got up. "You right, fam. Look I'm about to go back here and check on my girl and my baby. Thank y'all for being here, man. I don't know how I would get through this without you guys. O, tell your parents thank you, and I got them as soon as I get to the bank, brah," Trez said.

We dapped it up, and he hugged O, and then went to Emerald's room. O smiled and started to walk towards the exit of the hospital. "What you smiling for?" I asked, grabbing her hand.

"Because everything worked out, and I know after today my family will always be okay. First things first though, we need to find Santana's ass, and I mean as soon as possible."

"Oh you know I stay on that, but fuck all that. What are we about to go and do right now? I think you still owe daddy a few more rounds before the night is up, right?" I said, nibbling her ear walking behind us.

"Boy move, but I got you." She giggled.

We walked through the parking deck, and a Cadillac pulled in about two rows over from us. I watched as Ava got out the car with an older woman, and they went inside the hospital. "Babe, you see that shit?" I asked O, who was looking dead at her.

"You up, let's go," she said already following right behind them

They went to the nurse's station that we had just left from, and the older lady spoke up. "Yes, I need to find Emerald Daye."

Chapter Forty-One

TREZ

I sat by Emerald's beside listening to the baby monitor they had on her stomach blaring the baby's heart rate. I couldn't believe Emerald was pregnant and all I wanted was for her to wake up and tell me she was just as excited.

I didn't even care about her being that far along unless she was planning to get rid of it. I sat back and let her rest when the room door opened. When I saw Ava, I jumped up with my gun trained on her. She was followed by an older lady who didn't even look at Emerald when she walked in.

She didn't even care that I had my gun still trained on her as she walked up to me and just looked at me. "Man, I don't know who the fuck you are lady, but you need to move before I blow ya shit up," I said as she looked me all over.

"Quantrez Jones, my name is Charlene Jones," she said, and I slowly lowered my gun. I know she wasn't trying to come in here and say she was my mother.

"Okay, and what does that have to do with me? How do you even know my name anyway, and why are y'all in Emerald's room?"

"Trez, your father Rashad Jones had requested you come home.

Your mother had him kept away for too long, and he had to watch you grow from afar. But now, you are needed home."

I know this bitch was crazy because my mother passed away from a drug overdose when I was three. The city raised me, and I don't know why she felt that my father would hold any weight now, but she had me all the way fucked up. All that time in group homes and going house to house to finally being on the streets, and he just now coming for me when I got my shit together and things were working out for me.

"I don't know what this is, but I need y'all to walk out this room the same way you walked in— quietly. If my father would like to contact me, tell that deadbeat muthafucka that he needs to come himself," I said, and I looked back to Ava who was sitting over Emerald with tears in her eyes.

I was lost on why Ava would be crying for Emerald, and she didn't even know her. "Who did this to her?" Ava asked through clenched teeth.

"Man, I got this. How you know my girl anyway?" I asked.

"This is like my cousin. She grew up with my mother and me. Her parents left her with us to live the famous life until they died in a car crash. When my mother married your father, we took her in with us and raised her as my cousin. She was the closest thing to a sister I ever had," Ava said and, for some reason, I believed her.

"Avana, we don't have time for this. Let's go. She will be in good hands," Charlene said and looked back to me. "Your father has something for you, and when you're ready just open this, and everything you need to know is right there. Trez, he didn't stay away because he wanted to, and the only reason I am here is because I am part to blame for why he couldn't be in your life. I'm not asking you to forgive twenty-five years of absence, but just give him a chance to make up with his last years," she said and placed a pink and white flower on Emerald's bed.

I watched them leave and went to move the flowers. "No leave them there," I heard in a raspy voice. Looking down, I saw Emerald looking right back at me.

"Hey, babe. Take it easy. You took a few back there, didn't you?" I said, helping her lay back down and get comfortable.

"What the fuck happened, Trez?" she asked, looking just as pissed as me.

"Santana did this, but we are going to find her ass and make sure she pays. Any nigga who helped is going down too. Fuck the Lee family. You and the baby are fine though," I said, looking at her for signs that she knew.

When she looked at me like I had two heads, I knew she didn't know and finally, she looked down at her stomach and saw the monitors. "Oh my gosh, Trez, really?" she beamed, and I couldn't hold my smile back either.

"Yeah, you're going to be a mommy. You're twelve weeks along, and I think it's my junior brewing up in there." I laughed, making her giggle a little.

Just when I was about to ask her what was up with her aunt and cousin Ava, the room door opened again and in walked Amir and Tay. Tay looked like she wanted to kill somebody, and her eyes were set on Emerald.

"Fuck is up, Tay?" I asked, standing up.

"We saw Ava and some woman come in here looking for Emerald. Now, I know I'm new to this shit, but Ava is Bleek's baby momma, and that same bitch dropped Brandon off with not so much as a diaper in the middle of fucking winter, and we haven't seen the bitch since."

"Other than when she followed Bleek and Bella to the mall and thought nobody knew about it," Amir said, looking from me to Emerald.

I turned around and looked at Emerald for answers.

"Trez, they tried to get me to set you up, but I couldn't do the shit. Not because I fell for you, but because I fell in love with Simone. Your father is alive and well off might I add. He was in the middle of a war with the Lee family as well because one of the henchmen for Tao sent his sons to rob your father. That envelop tells you everything you need to know. I never lied, and I never crossed you, but I did make them think I was working with them."

I sat there taking in what she had just said to me. Here again, everything made sense. She was working with them to get me to go see him. That's why when I first met her she gave me the name Emily, making up the lie that she was really scared because of how I came off to her. I shook my head and couldn't believe this shit.

I had no plan of going to see my father or even getting to know him until I heard her mention the Lee family, and I know Tay and Amir were feeling the same way. "I will go see him and figure all of this out." I looked at Emerald. "I guess I now understand the whole point of Emily." I got my shit and walked out the room.

I couldn't trust Emerald's ass, and no matter how many time I give her to fix her lying ways, she continued to lie for no reason. I wasn't going to hold my kid down, and I wouldn't take Simone from her either, but I did have to get some things in order before I could even think about working things out with her. From this moment forward, I wanted to be with her, so I didn't ask for the ring back, but I did need my space. Maybe just for her to see what she is missing out on. Aside from Santana, I didn't date, so to get a ring from me was something special, and she didn't understand that. It took a lot for me to go to Tay and ask what she thought of her, but I did.

Fucked up in the head, I headed for my house to pack my things and go. While I was in my office, I came across a picture of Simone, Emerald, and I where Simone was looking at Emerald's stomach and smiling, and I never took any thought to that before now. I knew my baby girl deserved the best, and so do the child Emerald carried, but it would be a while before I could have a sit down with Emerald and work things out.

I closed my luggage and locked the house up. I went to Emerald's apartment and grabbed her a few items and things to wear while she was there. I was mad and hurt, but I was never petty. Emerald played me, but at the end of the day, she also held shit down for me when I did her dirty. After packing her things up, I went back to the hospital and gave her the clothes and also the food I bought on the way here. I found out that she could leave after the test results came back.

Tay agreed to let her stay with them while I was away, and I was cool with that. I need Em to keep a clear and level head going down there, and if she was with Tay, she was safe.

"We're going with you. The girls will all be at the new house, and the kids will be with our parents. You're not going alone, and you know this, brah," Amir said, stepping out into the hallway.

"I appreciate it, man," I said and dapped him up.

I didn't know what my father wanted, but I was on the way to find out. He better pray that when I get down there, his daughter doesn't find herself in Bleek's death grip. Sister and all, she was wrong for what she did and however, this played out was on her.

Chapter Forty-Two

SANTANA

I swung the door open and ran into the house. I had just let it rip, and the high I was on was amazing. Trez really thought he had won, and to be honest, I was aiming for his head the whole time. Emerald was really a bonus shot for me, and when I saw her ring, I lost it. The nigga never gave me a ring or even spoke on one, and I have his one and only child.

Stepping into the living room, I found my mother snorting a line. Getting on my knees beside her, I took my two lines and let the high take over me. I had been on this since fighting with Trez in the front yard. I was in so much pain that this was all that would help me cope.

"You need to get us some more before we leave. I don't like sharing these small sacks with your greedy ass," Mae slurred obviously more fucked up than me.

I didn't even reply. I had more things on my plate than she knew. I sat there staring at the wall thinking about my father, Tamia, and Maddison. I couldn't understand why Amir and Bleek would do what they did, and Trez of all people. He knew they meant the world to me, and if I could talk my family out of it, why couldn't they stay away too.

When my mother first told me, I didn't want to believe her. When she showed me the pictures, I couldn't hold back the rage and hate I had for them all. Tay knew, and Bella did too, and they let the shit happen. Even if they didn't know, they would all fall as casualties like my family did.

"Did you pick up some food while you were gone? You know ain't shit here to eat, and I gotta eat when I get high," Mae complained and was really blowing what little high I had left.

I couldn't move my body right now. I was numb to it all. All the hurt and the pain I felt wasn't nibbling at my heart anymore. I felt calm.

*

I woke up to the sound of a baby crying and thought it was Simone for a second. Shaking the thought from my head, I forced myself to get up and go get something to eat. Grabbing my keys, I was out the door and on the way to the grocery store.

By the time I finished shopping at Food Lion, I had decided I was too tired to cook, so Mae was going to have to take some Chinese food and a soda. I placed my order and sat in the corner of the restaurant and waited for my food. I was tired of dealing with my mother, and I no longer wanted anything to do with her selfish ass.

The more I sat and waited for my food, the more pissed off I got. When the man called me for my order, I snatched my bag and ran out the store. I sped all the way home just to let my mother know that after today she needed to find somewhere to go. Like when I was younger, if she wasn't going to put in any work, then she couldn't stay here living off me.

Walking into the house, it was quiet, and I could still hear her TV in the back room playing *Love & Hip-Hop* reruns. I placed the food in the kitchen and went to find the coke I had just picked up on the way here. I needed to get as high as I could before I did this.

Growing up, as bad as my mother was to me, all I ever wanted was to feel accepted and loved by her. Most of the time when I would getting trouble at home or at school, it was just so that I could have her attention without Soraya stealing all the shine. I wanted her to feel for me what she felt for Soraya. No, she wasn't always the perfect example, but she did at least try when it came to Soraya.

I got my lines out and ready to sniff and went in, getting a high I had never felt before. I was so energized that I ran into the pantry door trying to get to the rat poison and boric acid. I opened her rice and her chicken and sprinkled just enough maybe more, and sat the tops back over it. I went back to the living room and turned the TV on. I would just wait. She would be in the kitchen soon, yapping about food not being in the house, and she could thank me later for the meal.

≈

I woke up six hours later, and my TV had fallen asleep on my ass too. I stretched and sat up looking for my phone. I got the message I was waiting on and stood up to see if my mother had eaten yet.

Walking past the kitchen, I still saw the Chinese food bag sitting on the table right where I left it. Confused, I grabbed the bag and threw the food into the microwave and turned it on two minutes. "Ma!" I yelled and walked to the back of the house.

When I got to her room and opened the door, I couldn't believe the scene in front of my eyes. There was blood everywhere except on one wall where there was a note that was drawn on the wall.

Wrong Person
-Daddy

I shook my head in disbelief. How could they do my mother like this? She was sprawled out in the tub with her throat cut from ear to ear, and her tongue had been cut out. They had sliced her fingers, and she had thousands of cuts all over her body.

I suddenly heard sirens blaring in the distance, and I came back to reality. Grabbing what I could and packing it, I went into the garage and grabbed the gasoline cans and poured it all over the house and my mother's room. I didn't have much time, but I had to try and get this as far away from me as possible. I didn't know who killed my mother and how they got here, but to play saying daddy was sick. I jumped in my Toyota and hit the highway. I needed to get as far from this city as I could, but I had to make a stop first.

Sitting outside of Octavia's parents' house, I pulled my gun out and went to knock on the door. When her father came to the door, I smiled and waved.

"Hey, I came to see if the girls were still here?"

"Umm, no. They left with Octavia earlier," he said, and I knew he was lying. Pulling out my gun, I shot him right between the eyes.

Stepping over his body, I went searching for Simone and Amirah and heard them both crying in a nearby closet. When I yanked to door open, her mother stood there saying her final prayer. Since I wasn't completely heartless, I let her finish while I enjoyed a few yawns.

"Santana, you don't have to do this. Please, not in front of the kids!" she begged once she was done, but it fell on death's ears literally. I riddled her with so many bullets that I accidentally hit Simone by accident.

Dropping the gun, I rushed to pick up Amirah and looked over at my baby girl struggle to breathe. Covering her mouth and nose, I held my hand over her face firmly until she finally stopped breathing.

I had planned on having two meal tickets, but I could deal with just one. I grabbed Amirah's diaper bag and car seat and hit the road. I wanted to make sure Amir and Trez got my message, but more than anything, I wanted to make sure that Octavia and Bella knew that I knew their roles played in this as well.

Turning my radio on, I jumped on the high way and headed north. I took a few hits on the white, and like always, my sister came and told me to speed up.

"I need Amirah and you with me. Tana, hurry hit the gas harder," Raya said.

"I am, damn. I'm going as fast as I can go. We're coming," I said and pressed gas even harder.

I could hear Amirah screaming and crying, but I didn't let up. I was trying to hurry and get to Soraya because she needed us, and I finally was able to get her baby girl. Out of nowhere, I lost control of the car, and we started to spin.

Not caring anymore, I let the wheel go and enjoyed the whirl and wind until I felt us swirl into something, and everything went black.

To Be Continued

CPSIA information can be obtained
at www.ICGtesting.com
Printed in the USA
LVOW10s1535010318
568199LV00027B/1117/P